Bad Kansas

Winner of the Flannery O'Connor Award for Short Fiction

Bad Kansas

Stories by Becky Mandelbaum

THE UNIVERSITY OF GEORGIA PRESS   ATHENS

"Kansas Boys" first appeared in slightly altered form in
Great Jones Street. "Bald Bear" first appeared in slightly
altered form in *Salt Hill*.

Photograph p. iii by David Keller

© 2017 by the University of Georgia Press
Athens, Georgia 30602
www.ugapress.org
All rights reserved
Designed by Erin Kirk New
Set in 10/14 Warnock Pro

Most University of Georgia Press titles are
available from popular e-book vendors.

Printed digitally

Library of Congress Cataloging-in-Publication Data
Names: Mandelbaum, Becky, author.
Title: Bad Kansas : stories / by Becky Mandelbaum.
Description: Athens : The University of Georgia Press,
   [2017]
Identifiers: LCCN 2016056637 | ISBN 9780820351285 (pbk. :
   alk. paper) | ISBN 9780820351292 (e-book)
Classification: LCC PS3613.A52955 A6 2017 | DDC
   813/.6—dc23 LC record available at https://lccn.loc.
   gov/2016056637

for my mother

When I was in the second grade, my grandmother took me to Lawrence to raise me. And I was unhappy for a long time, and very lonesome, living with my grandmother. Then it was that books began to happen to me, and I began to believe in nothing but books and the wonderful world in books—where if people suffered, they suffered in beautiful language, not in monosyllables, as we did in Kansas.

—LANGSTON HUGHES

All we do is for this frightened thing
    we call Love, want and lack—
    fear that we aren't the one whose body could be
    beloved of all the brides of Kansas City,
    kissed all over by every boy of Wichita—
  O but how many in their solitude weep aloud like me—
  On the bridge over the Republican River
     almost in tears to know
     how to speak the right language—

—ALLEN GINSBERG, *Wichita Vortex Sutra*

Contents

Bad Kansas

Kansas Boys

When he was alive, Peter's dad had a dozen friends like Bob Deschutes—artists who'd gone to war and then returned to Kansas broken and restless, a milky film over their eyes. Once home, they nursed their wounds by devouring alcohol and fried food and telling stories that made their hearts ache more. Deschutes was, by these standards, one of Peter's dad's most quintessential buddies. He'd designed war recruitment posters in the late sixties before being placed in the field, where he lost a testicle and a hand, both on the left side. (Few people knew the real story, which was that he had lost the testicle years before, by antagonizing a fireman who, in a moment of unprofessional rage, aimed the fire hose at Deschutes's crotch.) Although naturally left-handed, Deschutes promptly declared himself ambidextrous and got to work painting a series of subpar and often wildly inappropriate portraits of children, most of them naked in a field of poppies. He preferred vodka in the mornings, wine once the sun went down.

Peter also knew that Deschutes had long ago loved the same girl as Peter's father—a dancer they'd referred to in drunken conversation as Slinky, either because they didn't want Peter's mother to hear the girl's real name or because saying it out loud hurt too much. The name came from a story in which the girl, wearing nothing but dime-store flip-flops and a cowboy hat, tumbled backward down a flight of stairs, breaking both of her big toes. These were stories from 1970s

San Francisco—somebody was always naked and falling. What Peter really wanted were stories about his father. Had he killed people? Had he watched children die? But his father was a private man and could hardly say "bless you" without straining an emotional muscle. It was Deschutes who had the stories and a loose mouth to go with them. All you had to do was feed him liquor and he'd spit out secrets like they were sunflower shells. Once—this was when Peter's father was still in the hospital—Deschutes took Peter aside and told him that his father may or may not have impregnated a woman in Vietnam. It was a warning: if word got to this woman that Peter's dad had died, she might come looking for money. At the time, Peter had cast it aside as a drunken joke. And yet, more than three years later, he still found himself waiting for a long-distance phone call, a letter addressed from across the world.

Peter hadn't seen Deschutes since his father's funeral, where Deschutes—wearing sunglasses and a powder-blue leisure suit—had burst out singing the chorus to "Free Bird" during the service, and so it came as a surprise when, on an otherwise ordinary Friday afternoon, the old man hobbled into the shirt store where Peter worked as a graphic designer. The job was a last resort for Peter, who had found no better use for his degree in graphic design since graduating the year before. Sometimes, when he thought about all of the T-shirts he'd borne into the world (BAD SPELLERS UNTIE, MY SPIRIT ANIMAL IS WHISKEY), he felt a deep sense of shame, as if he'd been caught masturbating outside an elementary school. He tried, mostly, not to think about it.

Deschutes charged toward Peter without a word of greeting and demanded a shirt with a princess on it.

"What kind of princess are we looking for?" Peter asked, hoping to make things quick. He had other work to do—design a logo for a kickball team, check the online orders—and besides, Deschutes depressed him. He had the same style as Peter's father: chambray shirts and abalone necklaces half-hidden by chest hair. He employed the same worn-out lingo: *Right on. Don't have a cow. Get real.* Even his mother had sometimes mistaken Deschutes for Peter's father—putting a hand on Deschutes's shoulder at a restaurant, handing him her purse (*Hold this for a second, will you?*), calling out to him, *Could you take a break from sitting on your ass and help me with the lawn mower?* Deschutes sucked his teeth. "It's for a little black girl. You got any black princesses?"

"Afraid not," Peter said, realizing how bad this sounded. "But I can make you one. We could sketch something right now if you wanted."

"You could do that for me?"

"It's part of what we do here."

Deschutes told Peter exactly what he wanted, down to the way the princess's hair should be braided. "Nothing too crazy, with those plastic bobble things. Just nice, simple braids."

Peter sketched the princess while the old man watched over his shoulder, the smell of his breath like an old metal spoon.

"You have good form," Deschutes said. "Good control. And eyes—they're natural for you. Took me years before I could do eyes. You wouldn't believe how many paintings I blew through, paintings of perfectly beautiful women whose eyes were dead, dead, dead. Might as well have given them doorknobs for eyes."

"My dad taught me," Peter said. Nobody, not even his art teachers, had ever complimented him on his eyes, though it had always been a secret source of vanity.

"You know," Deschutes said, "I could use some help around the house. I'm not in the best health these days. My fingers—the ones I got left—they go stiff. Doctor says it's arthritis, but I think it's more personal than that. My whole body's raging a war against me. Some days I can barely pick up a bar of soap." He paused, his face trembling. "That was a bad example. I don't need help in that way. Hygienic ways, I mean. I just need someone to do some housework. What do you think?"

"I'm actually pretty busy," Peter began, but the old man cut him off. "I'll pay you fifty dollars an hour."

Peter thought then of a girl with too many freckles and a lazy eye that showed if she turned her head all the way to the left. Her name was Rena, and she'd left Kansas only five days before to start a wilderness conservation program in Montana. She would be working in Yellowstone—a place Peter had only seen on postcards and in documentaries. She'd mentioned the program the winter before, as a sort of side note to a conversation they were having about national parks, but didn't bring it up again until a week before she was set to leave. She said she didn't tell him sooner because she didn't want their relationship to become a ticking time bomb. "I didn't want to think of everything as a matter of *This is last time we're together when it snows* or *This is the last time we're together for your birthday.*" She went on, listing all the lasts that had already occurred, unknowingly to Peter. "But *you* knew," he told her. "*You* knew they were the last time." And then the reality of what she was saying had hit him: she did not want to stay together. The conservation program was only five months long, stretching through the summer and part of the fall, but still she did not want to stay together. "I don't know where I'll be when it's over," she explained. "I don't know if I'll want to come back to Kansas." "You mean me," he said. "You don't know if you'll want to come back to me." She'd frowned the kind of frown one gives a homeless person, the kind that says, "There's nothing I can *really* do to help you."

Peter looked up and saw that Deschutes was waiting for a response. "When would you need me?" Peter asked, calculating the cost of a trip to Bozeman.

Deschutes cleared his throat. "Are you busy tonight?"

Deschutes lived twenty miles outside of Lawrence, in a little town called Vinland that was founded by abolitionists in the 1850s. More than a hundred years later, the town attracted a group of liberal army vets and became known as a sort of artists' colony where everybody secretly smoked pot and celebrated the solstice. A few residents taught art or philosophy at the university in Lawrence, but most were working artists. Some worked with neon, others with wood. The unifying factor was a sensibility not for art but for strangeness. The mayor made custom beaded handbags for celebrities but was better known for his collection of feral cats (his Special Kitty Crew) and for having once seen the Virgin Mary in an egg sandwich. One year, he tried to elect a blind sheep as sheriff—GIVE HIM THE BAAALOT!!! signs around town read. Despite its quirks, Vinland was not entirely removed from the traditions of small-town Kansas. There was a grain elevator and a small church, left over from the abolition days, as well as a diner where everything on the menu was either made of sugar or had once been alive. On the outskirts sat a modest airport where rich people from Lawrence and Topeka kept their prop planes. In the summertime, the planes wheezed overhead or did lazy loop the loops, their thick contrails staining the air, reminding the hippies below of the pleasures big money could buy.

Peter wished he had grown up in Vinland instead of in Lawrence, where nature was sectioned off into designated green spaces and being interesting entailed wearing small glasses and having a PhD in the humanities. What had his father been thinking? He'd been an artist, and yet he'd sold out, settling into a career designing greeting cards for Hallmark. Now, thinking of Rena out in the wilderness wearing Carhartts and sleeping in a tent (would she have her own tent or share one with people from her crew—possibly *male* people?), Peter regretted not having a more outdoorsy childhood, one where he'd learned how to start fires and identify edible plants instead of master Nintendo games and stick forks into electrical outlets.

Deschutes's house sat on top of a brown hill that overlooked both the church and the airport. The house was a squat structure with low ceilings and windows so choked with ivy that the light inside was dim and dappled. In any other hands, the house would have been morose and ugly, but Deschutes was an artist and had impeccable taste. He'd populated the house with antique clocks and Italian leather chairs and potted succulents boasting waxy red flowers. It was the type of home where men should have smoked pipes and discussed literature, but instead there was just Deschutes, doing whatever it was he did in his free time.

First thing, he led Peter to the kitchen and gave him a can of Old Style.

"I've always liked it out here," Peter said, looking around and sipping his beer. A stained glass window cast a box of red and purple light onto the hardwood floor between them. On the wall hung a poster of a naked woman riding a camel. It read: SMOKING IS SEXY.

Deschutes shrugged. "It can be nice anywhere, if you get the conditions right."

"But some places are nicer than others. By default."

"That's a myth told by the people who think they're unhappy because of where they are and not *who* they are. You ever lived outside Kansas?"

Peter thought of Rena and drank more beer. "No. Not yet."

"Well, you'll see."

Peter held his tongue and wondered if the old man was counting this as paid time. "So what's first on the agenda?" he asked.

Deschutes gestured for Peter to follow him. He went out the kitchen and up a skinny flight of stairs that creaked the whole way. The stairs opened up to a room that was all windows. Peter assumed it had once been a sleeping porch. He pictured turn-of-the-century children climbing into bed, a row of sheer white curtains inflating like the sails of ships. Now, the room smelled stale and the windows were painted shut, the glass frosted and cracked. The only wall without windows boasted a blank canvas. Scattered across the floor were dozens of charcoal portraits, all of a woman with big lips and small breasts: Slinky.

"My studio," Deschutes said, and went toward the far corner of the room, where one window met another. "You can see campus from here. Thought it would remind me that I'd escaped the academics." He took a moment to clear something from his throat and then gestured to the portraits on the floor. "I'll need you to pick the best one and put it on that canvas, if you don't mind."

Peter looked around, unsure whether he understood the old man right.

"Go ahead," Deschutes said. "Pick which one you like best."

Peter scanned the portraits at his feet. There were too many to consider all at once. In some, Slinky's face filled the entire paper, her eyes the size of mangos. In others, she was far away—reclining on a sofa, wrapped in a shawl near a fire hydrant. There were traces of color, a splash of peach on her cheeks or a blur of green where her foot touched the earth.

"Go on," Deschutes said. "Don't be precious."

"I thought I'd be doing housework. Cleaning. Or maybe mowing the lawn."

"This is housework. We're in my house. Painting is work. Remember, I'm paying you."

Peter recalled a vision of Rena on a summer night the year before, her head in his lap as they lay on a quilt in a friend's backyard, watching a group of neighborhood kids dart after fireflies. "We could have a kid one day," she'd said, more as a revelation than a proposition. It had scared him at first, but then he'd gotten used to it, started imagining a little girl with Rena's eyes. He could teach her how to draw. Rena could teach her how to garden.

Peter began to sort through the charcoals, creating a stack of the ones he preferred. He liked them all, but he knew some would take longer to paint than others. When he was done, he had two piles. He closed his eyes and thumbed through the yes pile, finally pulling a corner at random. When he opened his eyes he was holding a sketch in which Slinky was naked but for a string of pearls. All around her, peacock feathers shot up from the earth, some the size of trees.

"This one," Peter said, holding the paper by a corner, so as to not smudge the charcoal.

Deschutes nodded.

Peter was excited to sort through the old man's oil paints, which he knew would be of higher quality than any he could afford. He wondered if Deschutes had ever used the same oils as his father—the ones eventually linked to his bladder cancer. Then he wondered if Slinky knew about his father's death, if either man had kept in contact with her over the years. The thought of bringing her to life, this woman who had been shared by his father and Deschutes, seemed a more interesting way to spend his time than mowing grass or pulling weeds. He wondered what Rena was doing, and then, indulging in this thought, imagined her watching him as he cleaned the brushes, chose his colors, and began to carefully mix the paints.

Deschutes watched him work. At one point he disappeared from the room and returned with a bottle of wine, the skin above his lips stained purple. He did not offer any to Peter, and Peter was glad for it—he wanted to focus all of his attention on Slinky, who was slowly taking form on the canvas. The two did not speak, except for once when Deschutes sneezed and Peter offered a quiet "bless you" that the old man acknowledged with a quick humming sound.

At sunset, Deschutes disappeared again. Peter heard a toilet flush and then the old man was back with a new bottle of wine tucked under his arm and a stack of yellowed papers in his hand.

"What are those?" Peter asked.

"Letters. From her. Keep painting."

Peter returned to his work as Deschutes cleared his throat and began to read:

Dear Honey Bear:

I miss you more each day. Feels like since you left, everyone looks like a lump of coal. You'll never guess what happened at the Sizzle last night. Some guy choked on a butterscotch and dropped dead. Can you believe it? Everyone thought he was just drunk, but then come closing we find him on the ground, blue as a berry. He'd probably been dead for hours. Had a picture of some toddlers in his pocket. Little twins with yellow hair. I thought about how if I died right this minute, people would find a picture of you.

Love, Slinky

"She loved me, all right," Deschutes said, more to himself than Peter.

"Why didn't you stay with her?"

Deschutes took a sip of wine, closed his eyes. "San Francisco was expensive—we didn't have jobs. So when your dad found work for us in Lawrence, in the card business, I followed him." He licked his lips, as if tasting the decision. "I was a chickenshit, so I followed him."

"Why didn't she come with?"

The old man laughed. "You can't take a girl from California and stick her in Kansas. It'd be like putting a fish in a tree."

"Sounds like she would have come with if you'd have asked her."

"Well, I didn't ask her." He stared out at the ground, and then yawned, his whole body shuddering. "How about you come back tomorrow," Deschutes said. "Don't get up early or anything. Just come when you feel like it."

Peter already knew that he would set an alarm so he could do a sunrise drive through the country. He went as if to shake Deschutes's hand but realized that the old man's only hand was occupied by the letters. What remained of his left hand was concealed by a shirtsleeve pinned shut at the end. Peter wondered how long it had taken Deschutes to adjust to the missing hand, how long before he'd learned to reach with the right instead of the left. Someone once told him that it took half the length of a relationship to get over a breakup. A hand seemed like an equally dramatic loss, but Peter couldn't be sure. A hand did not disappear intentionally, to spite the arm, nor was there the maddening possibility that it might someday return.

That night, Peter called Rena. No answer. It was possible she was on a hitch. She'd explained her schedule before she left, how her crew would spend ten days in the backcountry followed by six days in Bozeman, where they would share a cheap apartment. He'd been keeping track of the days but it was possible something had changed—perhaps they'd left early. Perhaps she was already in the wilderness, even further out of reach.

He kept his phone by his side as he looked up flights from Kansas City to Bozeman. From a single night of painting he could afford more than half the plane ticket. He would need a couple hundred dollars more, to cover whatever he wouldn't be making at the shirt store while he was gone, as well as some extra cash for food, and maybe a motel room or two along the way, if things with Rena went sour. He would not tell her he was coming but would instead show up bearing flowers, or a box of those expensive French caramels she liked from the co-op, or maybe both. He would do what he could and then hope for the best. Fifty years from now, he would not have to wonder: *What if?*

In the morning, Peter filled a Thermos with coffee and made the drive to Vinland. He put the windows down and hung his arm out like he used to as a kid, feeling the texture of the air. Over the course of the drive, the sky went from deep gray to purple, finally settling on a soft white the color of paper.

At the house, Deschutes was making pancakes—an awkward procedure with only one hand. "I'll feed you breakfast," he told Peter, "but lunches are your own responsibility."

Peter sat down and drank the rest of his coffee. He hadn't thought he was hungry, but he ate four pancakes with syrup and butter. Deschutes did not eat but instead watched Peter, occasionally drinking from a mason jar of orange juice that smelled strongly of vodka. Rena used to watch Peter eat, when she was on a juice cleanse or was just, to use her words, feeling bloated. She'd follow Peter's food from fork to mouth, fork to mouth. Peter hadn't thought twice about it— he'd taken it as a sign of love.

When the food was gone, Deschutes led Peter upstairs. Peter loved returning to a new project, reassessing the details he'd forgotten or misremembered during his time away. But the portrait of Slinky looked exactly as he recalled, every line and shadow in its place. He took his time preparing his tools and mixing his paints—he needed to kill time.

"How did you meet her?" Peter asked.

Deschutes grunted and looked up from the book he was reading, a *Farmer's Almanac* from 1977. "Your dad never told you?"

"He never told me anything. I think he was afraid I'd tell my mom."

Deschutes was quiet for a moment. "She wasn't a whore, if that's what you're thinking."

"I wasn't thinking she was anything."

"Good. Because she was a teacher. Eventually she was a dancer— that's when we met her—but before that she was a teacher. In San Francisco."

"Why'd she stop teaching?"

Deschutes set his book face down on the floor. "She had an accident—bus hit her while she was riding her bike. Screwed up her brain so she couldn't keep her numbers straight. And then her body was all banged up so her fiancé left her—said he didn't want to spend his life fucking an invalid. She had tragedy coming out her eardrums. You could see it when she danced." He looked at the canvas and smiled. "Obviously, everyone was in love with her. She had a waist so small you could fit your hands around her, and she always smelled like flowers. Not to mention she was smart as hell. Even after the brain damage, she could memorize a page of poetry in one sitting."

"That's why you liked her? Because she smelled good and memorized poems?"

"Well, sure. That's what men liked back then. I see what you're thinking. The girl I got now—she's nothing in the way of looks. But she treats me like a house cat and that's what matters. At this age, it's about being cared for."

Peter turned his attention to his painting. He thought of all the things he loved about Rena: How she wouldn't take a bite of food until she'd offered a taste to everyone around her. How if someone gave her a book she always read it, no matter how much she disliked it. Once, he woke in the middle of the night and found her sitting at the window, watching an incoming thunderstorm. He loved her more for wanting this moment of romance to herself, and yet he'd felt jealous, left out. And now she was gone, experiencing everything by herself, taking the world in without him. She was braver than he was.

"My new girlfriend is black," Deschutes was saying. "Did you know that?"

"I didn't."

"Her name is Harmony. She's got a big singing voice and a certification in music therapy. Her daughter's name is Sierra. That's who the T-shirt's for. She loves princesses even though her mom tells her not to believe in them." He paused again, considered the painting. "Harmony's prettier than Slinky in some ways. Mostly when I'm not looking at her."

"Won't this painting bother her?"

"Harmony doesn't care about that. The past."

"Has she seen this room? The charcoals?"

Deschutes made a sniffling sound and looked away from Peter, meaning that no, she did not know about the room or Slinky. "I always figured people got over things like this, these old crushes. It's been what, forty years? Still I'm like a little boy with Slinky."

"But what about Harmony? Don't you love her?"

"Sure I do. But I need somebody more. I need somebody to want me. To touch me. It's been a long time since anyone's touched me."

"You and Harmony don't—you know?"

Deschutes shook his head. "She's got pains in her joints. And she vowed when her husband died that she'd never please another man. We're partners in a spiritual way. It's not enough, but it's something."

Peter's stomach churned. He did not want to think of the old man in anything but a spiritual relationship.

"I've got an idea," Deschutes was saying. "Let's take a little field trip. My treat. You ever heard of the Outhouse?"

Peter had. The Outhouse was a gentlemen's club on the outskirts of Lawrence. He'd gone there his freshman year with a group of guys he'd long since lost touch with. The club was housed in a big white building that had been a bank in the thirties. The club owner had installed little cages into the alcoves where the tellers used to stand. If you were drunk enough and stood close enough to the cages, you couldn't tell who was inside and who was out. The girls were not pretty, but the lights were kept low and happy music made everything seem less sad.

Five minutes later, they were in Peter's car. Peter did not want to go, but he wanted the money, and Deschutes seemed set on getting out of the house. Neither of them considered that the club would not be open midmorning on a Saturday.

"They don't open for another hour," Peter explained to Deschutes. They were standing outside the building, reading a sign posted on the club's front door, which was locked.

"But I see the girls right there!" Deschutes said, and pointed to two women who were sharing a cigarette by a Dumpster. The women turned to give him a nasty look. "Let us in," Deschutes yelled.

"Sorry, honey," one of the girls said. She had big front teeth and red hair that came down to her waist. "We gotta get everything prepped and ready."

"But I'm ready and I'm the customer," Deschutes said. "And the customer's always right."

Peter took the old man by the arm and attempted to lead him back toward the car. "Come on," he said. "We can come back later."

"I'm not a child," Deschutes said, yanking his arm away. He stormed up to the women, pulling his wallet from his pocket along the way. He waved it in their faces saying, "Do your job. I'm a United States veteran."

The women stepped away and began to shout at Deschutes. One of them went and pounded on a back door to the club, calling for somebody named Big Rick. Deschutes began throwing bills at the girls, who swatted them away while giggling.

Seconds later, a bald man with a neck like a Greek column came rushing out. "What's going on here?" he asked.

Peter stepped up and stood between Deschutes and Big Rick. "Don't worry, we're leaving."

"That's what I thought," Big Rick said, and waited until Deschutes and Peter were in the car before taking out his own cigarette, which he sucked down like a man who had just made love. The girls scrambled to collect the money at their feet.

In the car, Deschutes banged a fist against the dashboard. "Bunch of sluts," he said. "What's it matter what time the club opens? A body's a body, whether it's nine in the morning or ten at night." He looked at Peter, his eyes wild with desperation. "You don't know what it's like— to go years without being intimate with a woman. I feel half-alive. And then this hand." He held his left arm before his face and shook it. "It's like God didn't want me to be with anybody anymore. I don't know what I did wrong. I don't know why the rest of the world gets to love but I don't."

"You have a girlfriend," Peter said. He was trying not to get angry—he was embarrassed by the scene at the club. "Why isn't that enough? Some people don't even have that. Some people have nobody." *Like me*, he wanted to say.

"What do you know about anything? You're just a boy. Too scared to take what you want. Just like your father—he probably could have had Slinky, but he settled for your mom. I told him he was making a mistake, that she'd get fat once she had kids. You could see it in her bone structure. Was I wrong?" He looked at Peter, as if genuinely expecting an answer.

"That's my mother you're talking about."

"Exactly. You know what she looks like." There was a moment of silence and then he said, "I'm starving all of a sudden. Let's grab a burger. Or tacos."

"I'm taking you home," Peter said, and then turned up the radio as loud as he could stand it.

A memory came to him as he drove. He was young, maybe five or six, and Deschutes was over for a barbecue. His father must have been out back doing something—starting the grill or messing with the sound system—because it was just Peter's mother and Deschutes in the kitchen, where Peter sat at the table, pulling the tops from strawberries. From where he sat, he could see his mother and Deschutes at the sink, making kebabs. One moment, the two of them were talking, laughing. The next, Deschutes's hand was between Peter's mother's legs, inching up and up. She sucked in air but did not, as Peter expected, pull away from the hand. She closed her eyes, leaned against the counter.

Peter's first instinct was to call his father and tell him about the memory. Where had it come from? How could he have forgotten it for this long? When this passed—as it always did—he wasn't sure what to do. He couldn't look at Deschutes. He was afraid he might hit him.

Back at the house, Deschutes grabbed a bottle of wine and headed upstairs. Unsure of what else to do, Peter followed. He didn't feel like painting, but the old man was stationed in his usual spot, his gaze fixed to the canvas.

"You'll finish it today," Deschutes said, a command rather than a question.

Peter tried to stay calm. "I think I'm done here."

"What are you talking about? You don't even have her eyes."

"I guess you'll have to do them yourself."

Deschutes licked his lips. "You finish it today or I'm not paying you for any of it."

Peter tried to calm himself, but he thought of Rena, of the cost of the flight. "We had a deal. You said you'd pay if I worked and I did."

"I don't see any contract," Deschutes said, wiping some spittle from his chin. "I don't remember signing anything. Do you?"

Peter thought about hitting the old man but knew he couldn't. Deschutes was too old, and his dad's buddy, and a veteran. And so he went first for the love notes, which he stuffed into his back pocket, and then for the canvas.

"Just like your dad," the old man said. "Always running away. A coward."

"Get over yourself," Peter said, and then took off down the stairs, faster than he knew Deschutes could go.

The canvas barely fit in the backseat of his car. Peter had to force the door shut, but eventually it closed, sealing the half-finished Slinky inside. Before starting the engine, Peter glanced up and saw Deschutes in the window of the sleeping porch, watching.

At home, Peter left Slinky in the car. He wanted her to suffocate, to melt into the canvas and then into his car's upholstery.

Not wanting the comfort of the couch, Peter sat on the floor and started to read the love notes, which were yellowed from age and thin as onionskin. Slinky's writing was small and faint and difficult to read—she had written with a pencil. As he read, he was surprised to find that nearly all of the letters mentioned his father. To Peter, his father had always been Donald, but back then he must have been Donnie. A nickname, Peter thought. His father had a nickname.

One note stuck out in particular.

Dear Bobby,

I keep thinking back to that time you and Donnie and me went out to that beach up north of here. The one with the sea lions? Donnie said something like, "What if the whole universe was built just for the two of us?" I was so fucked up I couldn't tell if he meant the two of us as in me and him or you and him—like maybe the universe was made for the two of you guys to go around pillaging the city, and I was just part of that package. An asterisk. I want to know but then again I don't—I couldn't stand to be Donnie's asterisk.

The letters went on like this, addressed to Deschutes but speaking mostly of Peter's father. He kept reading and discovered that Slinky had eventually married. Had two children. Out of need, she said. Not love. Still, she missed her Kansas boys. She missed her Donnie.

He thought then about Rena, about all of the things they would never do together, not because of distance or location or timing, but because she did not love him. Hadn't he known it all along? Hadn't he seen it in the way she never quite looked at him when she said she loved him—her gaze always off in the distance, as if the man she really loved were standing just behind him? Or how she had asked her best friend, Tori, to take her to the airport? He'd told himself it was because she didn't want a maudlin good-bye scene, but now he could admit the truth: she didn't want him to be the last person she saw in Kansas. It really was that simple: there was love, and there was the absence of love. The heart was not a sunset but a light switch. He wondered whether somebody would ever come and switch his off, or if he'd end up like Deschutes—trapped in a fluorescent room, wanting desperately to sleep.

He crumbled the letters and threw them away. A headache pressed against his neck and cheeks, and so he swallowed a Tylenol from a bottle Rena had left behind. He let a moment pass, and then he removed the letters from the trash, smoothed them out, and placed them between the pages of a thick anthology of essays called *How Nature Can Heal Us*, which Rena had given him when they'd first started dating. He told himself he'd return the letters to Deschutes in the morning; it was the right thing to do. Perhaps he would also apologize, return the painting. Perhaps the old man would forgive him and allow him to finish the painting for the full sum of money. Perhaps he could still buy the plane ticket. Perhaps nothing had been lost after all.

At last he got into bed, deciding to sleep everything away. The covers still smelled like Rena, like the almond lotion she rubbed onto her elbows before going to bed. He breathed in deep, imagining her beside him. She would turn to him and smile, her hair cascading over the pillows, which still held the scent of her coconut shampoo. He wondered, with a sinking feeling, if it would ever be a good time to wash them.

The Golden State

As these things go, we left Kansas on the hottest week of the year. A red rash burned over the weather map as Alec and I shoved everything we owned Tetris-style into a U-Haul, which we then dragged across the prairie and desert, completely bypassing the pretty parts. In Denver I suggested a day hike, but Alec ruptured his Achilles tendon playing Ultimate Frisbee in college (an injury I never entirely believed), so anything athletic was strictly out of the question.

The drive carried on, all garbled talk radio and forest green mile markers and Alec listing off things we needed to do once we got to California: buy a box fan, change our mailing address, get a parking permit. Boring, boring, boring. Around Vegas I asked if he'd ever go hiking with me. He turned to look at me, revealing soft pockets of darkness under his eyes. He hadn't slept the night before—at dawn I found him sitting upright in the hotel bed reading *Les Misérables*, shoveling ranch-flavored corn nuts into his mouth.

"You're free to go hiking without me," he said.

"But I want to go *together*."

"We'll do other things together." He was using his lecherous voice—he reached over and squeezed my thigh. "Did I mention I'm glad you're coming with me?"

"Well, nobody wants to move alone."

He kept his eyes on the road. "That is the kind of comment I will choose to ignore."

I was not without a point. So far, he'd seen to it that the move lacked all romance. He put a deposit down on the house in California without consulting me and then fell asleep an hour into our going-away party, snoring away on the sofa as my friends and I danced to "Girls Just Want to Have Fun" on the coffee table beside him. Most of our conversations over the past few weeks had revolved around how to best pack his dishware. At one point I asked if he thought I was his assistant. "If you were my assistant," he said, "I'd be paying you."

I turned and watched the desert spit out tumbleweed. It was just like in the spaghetti westerns, all red sand and saguaros. About every other minute a semi came hurtling past us, plastic truck nuts swinging from the trailer hitch.

Already, I missed Kansas.

California was supposed to be better in every way: better food, better weather, better people. In movies, the West Coast was a utopia of beaches and liberal politics, hippies high-fiving scientists at the farmers market. Meanwhile, redwoods and cheap tacos and Yosemite! My Kansas friends feigned jealousy, although they too were heading out for other lands: Madrid, Seattle, a rustic lodge in the Rocky Mountains.

Alec had his own campaign, whose main platform was that California was not Kansas: no snowstorms or tornados or governors trying to arm children with rifles. Plus, he'd gotten a job near Sacramento, teaching French literature at a university. The job didn't pay well, but it was—back to his main point—very much not in Kansas.

The university town was not by water or mountains, but somewhere vaguely between—the Central Valley. "It's the best of both worlds!" Alec promised. He had promised many things over the course of our relationship: that he would only smoke cigarettes after sundown, that I could borrow his car without asking so long as I was sober, that he would love me ferociously. This was his word: *ferociously*. So far, he'd made good on everything, which I credited to his advanced age. He was twelve years older than me and had been my French teacher.

Technically he was a lecturer—he had his eyes on tenure that would likely never be his, because as much as he wanted to be French, the truth was that his real name was Alex and he came from a poor farming town in upstate New York where people ate pigs' feet and married their first cousins. That his life and career were turning into something of a failure was entirely his problem, and yet sometimes it felt like my own. I'd just graduated with a degree in linguistics and couldn't think of anything better to do than follow him. What was a young woman supposed to do with her life? The answer probably should have been: Anything! Everything! She's politically liberated! But something in my gut—perhaps fear masquerading as love—was urging me to stick with Alec. Plus, I had very little money.

"You're making a big mistake" was what my mother told me.

"But I'm in love," I said.

"Love has weak legs. You'll see."

I told her I'd prove her wrong, but I could hear the uncertainty in my voice. At this point, the doom feelings were compacted into a small kernel, located somewhere behind my belly button.

Our house in the Central Valley cost three times more than the one-bedroom we'd shared in Lawrence and was, I should mention, not really a "house." Granny cottage, they called it—whoever *they* were. At best, it was a room in which someone had accidentally left a sink and a toilet. At worst, it was an architectural side note to the larger, two-story mission-style home in which a history professor and a veterinarian lived with their litter of blond offspring. We were there to help pay the mortgage.

Inside, Alec's head scraped against the ceiling, where a network of cobwebs stretched from corner to corner like prayer flags. In the kitchen, I put my arms out and twirled like a ballerina, my fingers grazing the cabinets. There were two rooms, one of which was the bathroom. An image came to my mind of a mastiff and a dachshund forced into a gerbil cage.

"Cozy," Alec said, and forced a smile that read: *Do not panic or girlfriend will panic.*

I said, "As a womb. Or a very, very small, overpriced home."

We got to work unpacking and ended up making okay-but-sort-of-forced love on the kitchen linoleum. This is how we discovered the cockroaches. I'd never seen one up close before. Kansas had all sorts of critters—millipedes, brown recluses, cicadas—but nothing as Kafkaesque as a cockroach. Like a rotted thumbnail with legs.

"They say when the world ends, it'll just be all cockroaches and Twinkies," Alec said. He was naked, dust on his thighs.

"Where do you want to be when the world ends?" I asked.

He stared up at the ceiling, thinking. "Maybe the ocean. Watching the waves." He turned to look at me. "What about you?"

There was only one answer I could think of, and because I didn't know better, I figured it must be the truth. "I'd want to be right here," I told him. "With you."

Alec started school and I started researching the state of California, specifically the Central Valley. I had the time—the days had begun to stretch outward in all directions, expanding along with the cosmos. The mornings were temperate but by noon the house was an inferno; there was no air-conditioning unit (the house being not really a house), and so I grew to worship the monstrous box fan that stood by the window, whirring like a jet engine. At night, Alec grew damp with sweat so that sleeping with him was like sleeping with a man-sized baked potato. My time in bed was spent wrestling with the sheets, dreaming of house fires and prairie burns. Most of my REM cycles came in the languid afternoons, when I'd fall into naps deep as a miner's hole. When I woke up—startled by the sound of an ambulance or the feeling of sweat gliding across my stomach—I had to crawl my way back to reality, back to the scorching surface of my new life.

My research paid off in a bad way. I learned that California was running out of water, that there were too many people compressed into too little space too far from natural water sources. Even in Kansas, I'd been complicit: the production of a single California walnut required five gallons of water, and I liked to eat my walnuts by the handful.

I learned that the college town had played host to a series of freak tragedies: stranglings, decapitations, body parts Saran Wrapped and left in Dumpsters. Even nature seemed bent on retaliation. More than four people had died after driving into the same eighty-year-old magnolia tree. Further research suggested the tap water might cause organ cancer and that rabid bats roamed the treetops after sundown.

Where had Alec brought me? Better question: Why had I let him?

The first week, Alec came home before dinnertime, tired and grumpy. His office was hot, and the students were stupid.

"I thought this was supposed to be a world-class public university," I said.

He brought a tub of mint chip ice cream from the freezer and hacked at it with a fork. He was on a medicine that made him crave sugar—on more than one occasion I'd caught him in bed at dawn, a salad bowl of Lucky Charms in his lap. "They're just rich kids who want to stay rich," he said. "All they really want to do is design drugs or build robots. They just need my class for the language credit."

"You're saying not one of them actually cares about learning a new language?"

Something flickered in his eyes, a premonition of danger. "There's one girl—her father's a diplomat. She already knows Italian and Spanish. It's like teaching a fish to drink water."

"A girl?"

He shoveled more ice cream into his mouth. "Don't worry, she's probably gay. They're all gay here. Or Marxist."

I grabbed the tub of ice cream, brought it to my face, and licked the surface.

"Gross," Alec said, yanking the tub from me. "What's the matter with you?"

"It's mine," I said, pointing to the ice cream. "Everything I touch is mine."

He winced. Sometimes this happened: I played baby, he played dad. "Have you thought about looking for a job?" he said. "They're hiring at the cafeteria."

"I have a degree in *linguistics*."

"And my barista has a PhD in philosophy. Get over yourself." He stood and took the ice cream to the living room, which meant he relocated it about a yard east of the kitchen table.

"I want to take a class," I called to him. "I'm wasting my potential here."

He did not look at me but instead turned on the television. "It's your life. Do what you want."

I decided that academia was stupid, and so I signed up for a woodworking class I planned to pay for with the rent money I would withhold from Alec. I'd recently read an article in the *New Yorker* about a novelist who claimed to have learned everything she needed to know about writing from her years laying brick in Indiana. Surely woodworking would open up some dusty cellar door in my soul, revealing a room of glittering treasure.

The class was held in a Presbyterian church. I thought of Jesus and Santa's elves and wooden crosses, wondering if there was something inherently spiritual about carpentry, or if Jesus just happened to be good at making stuff.

I'd expected plaid-wearing twenty-somethings, but the class was mostly old men and New Age moms. We started with introductions. When I said I was from Kansas the class let out a collective coo, as if I'd admitted to being a puppy with a serious case of kennel cough. "You're sure not in Kansas anymore," one of the old men said. An invisible puppeteer gathered his wrinkles and pulled his face into a horrifying grin.

We were starting with birdhouses. Our teacher was a middle-aged man with a red beard and hands like two T-bone steaks. He came up behind me and showed me how to sand down the edges of my wood. Inhaling his aftershave, I pressed my butt into the crotch of his blue jeans and closed my eyes, thinking all the while about the diplomat's daughter. Was she skinny? Blond? Could she build a birdhouse out of scrap wood? The teacher cleared his throat and went to help one of the moms beside me. After class, he handed me my tuition check and said it'd be best if I didn't return. *Prude*, I thought, and ripped up the check.

Outside, a boy from class was waiting near the curb. "What'd you think?" he asked. He was young, maybe my age, with a hipster mustache and a tan baseball cap that said BLUEHORN WINERY.

"Not for me. I decided to quit."

"Same. I already know half the stuff anyways—I just figured it'd be a good way to meet people. You know?" He smiled in a way that suggested I was the people. He then asked if I wanted a ride. A nearby bank sign read 104 degrees, so I followed him to his rusted Civic. A sticker on the bumper read KEEP TAHOE BLUE. Inside, something had eaten away a golf-ball-sized hole in the floor. As he drove, I watched the road go by between my feet.

"So are you digging it out here so far?" he asked.

I realized it was the first time anybody had asked me this. Even Alec had avoided the question, perhaps to avoid an answer that might require some action on his part. "Not really," I said. "I know that may be hard to imagine."

"Not at all. I understand—you're homesick."

"I'm not homesick."

"Then what are you?"

"I'm just not comfortable here. I'm not a Californian."

"Maybe you should go to the ocean," he said. "That's what all the fuss is about. Check out Point Reyes if you get the chance."

We were at the "house" already. He pulled over and let the car idle so that he could jot his name and number onto an In-N-Out napkin. Theo was his name. "I work the farmers market if you're ever around," he said. "I'm the honey man."

"Honey man," I said. "That's sweet."

He was blushing as I got out of the car. Inside, I put the In-N-Out napkin next to the toaster, so that Alec would find it.

The next day, I dropped Alec on campus and took his car to Point Reyes. The drive was all metal and tension. Aside from the traffic, the road kept curving and expanding and turning into bridges. In Kansas, you could close your eyes and take your hands off the wheel. Count to fifteen Mississippi.

I found a trailhead and walked a handful of miles until the Pacific appeared on my left. *Holy shit*, I thought, *that doesn't end until Japan.* There was blue water and wheat-colored sand and cliffs taller than the tallest building in Wichita. Land, I now saw, was like pie. Who would settle for just the middle when the crust was the whole point? I felt bad for Kansas, that everything in it was the same: land, land, land. The occasional mosquito-infested watering hole. And then me, my family, all my history, and everyone I'd ever loved. If there was a map that glowed in the places where I'd loved and been loved, it would burn bright in the center, surrounded by darkness. Perhaps a lazy squiggle would mark the route Alec and I took on I-70. Perhaps not.

I scrambled down the trail to a waterfall. This close to the water, I felt the first inkling of claustrophobia. It occurred to me that the openness of the sea was a lie: the ocean was not space, it was the opposite of space! It was a wall, a cage, a no-man's-land promising imminent death.

Nearby, a group of people had congregated around a beached seal. It took me a while to realize that something was wrong with it. It was craning its neck in a sickly way, as if trying to break itself in half. Without warning, it began to convulse. White foam streamed from its mouth as quickly and voluptuously as soft serve. It was going to die, and these people were going to watch it.

"It's having an orgasm!" a young man yelled.

Around him, the women squealed in joyful disgust. One raised her phone to take a picture.

Leave it alone! I wanted to shout, but had the ridiculous suspicion they would turn to me and know I was from Kansas. *You're not even from here*, someone, probably the kid wearing the pink bandana, would say. *This is just how we do things. It's ocean stuff. You wouldn't understand.*

Later that night, Alec laughed when I told him the story. We'd just made love and were in bed, face to face. He'd been sweet that evening, making lasagna for dinner and then massaging my feet, which were sore from the hike. After dessert, we unpacked a box of candles and lit them in the bedroom. It smelled like our apartment in Lawrence: vanilla and mint. In many ways, it was the best night we'd had in the house yet.

"Your friends used to shoot squirrels with pellet guns," he reminded me. "You didn't find them morally bankrupt."

"That's different. These people at the beach were malicious. And anyways, those guys used to make squirrel stew."

"Squirrel stew isn't a thing."

"I'm telling you—they made stew. They weren't killing for sport."

"All right. Your friends made stew. Either way, you just hate the people here because you think you're tougher than them."

"I do not."

"You do. You think they're soft because they eat avocados and go surfing. And like you're some hardened warrior just off the Oregon Trail."

"None of that's true!" I regretted raising my voice. I wanted to stay nice, for the evening to retain its kind trajectory. The mint candle was still burning on the nightstand, casting a friendly orb of light onto the wall. *Help me, candle*, I thought. *I'm losing him.*

"Have you discussed any of this with the napkin man?" Alec asked.

My stomach dropped—I'd forgotten about the napkin. About Theo. I wanted to undo it, to take it back and throw it in the trash. "I don't know anything about a napkin man."

"You don't know anything about that napkin on the counter?"

"I do not."

"Did you think I wouldn't call the number?" He looked at me hard, unblinking. "You fuck with me, I'll fuck with you back."

The words made my throat ache. "That's not a nice way to talk to the one you love."

"I'm tired," he said, turning away from me. "Some of us went to work today."

I held my tongue, pressed my fingernails into my palms, where they left little frowns of pain.

If Alec wanted me to work, I would work. For the rest of the week, I swept and mopped and ran Q-tips along the baseboards. Once everything was spotless, I started cooking elaborate meals that smelled so good Alec had no choice but to eat them. On Friday, I thought I'd try the farmers market, which blossomed in the center of town in the evening, while Alec held office hours.

I walked along the crowded produce stalls, making a point to eat as many samples as possible. I touched everything I could, running a lazy hand along phalanxes of pluots and cabbages. Like he promised, Theo was at the honey table, surrounded by plastic bears filled with golden liquid. We made a plan to meet at the ice cream stand a half hour later, when he had a break. Before moving on to the pickle stand, I tapped the cap of every honey bear on display.

As it turned out, Theo had turned twenty-three since I last saw him. He bought me a scoop of coconut ice cream with one of the two-dollar bills his grandmother had sent him for his birthday. She lived in Oregon. Every year she sent him fifty two-dollar bills and a nickel for good luck.

"I've heard nice things about Oregon," I told him. Cone in hand, I was steering him away from the market, toward campus. Toward Alec.

He looked at me like I'd just mentioned his childhood best friend. "I *love* Oregon. My dream is to start an organic farm outside of Portland. I have loads of friends who live there. They just love it. There's so much to do, and the food's incredible." He went on like this, as if Portland were paying him to advertise.

"Why don't you just go there, then?"

It seemed the thought had never occurred to him. "I don't know. I mean, I'd need to find a place. Save some money. I guess it just doesn't seem like the right time." He glanced shyly at me and smiled. I pulled him toward the French building, where Alec happened to be walking out with a redhead. She wore a white bow in her hair, like a dove had flown into her head and died there.

Alec saw us from across the courtyard and shot me a nasty look. "This the napkin man?" he called.

"Only if that's the diplomat's daughter," I called back, and then pulled Theo back toward the market. The moment was over before it even began.

After a few minutes of silence, Theo said, "Was that your dad?"

I usually laughed at this type of question, but now it just made me sad. "Yes," I said. "That was my dad."

"I didn't know you moved here with your family."

"I did—we're very close."

"He looks like Vin Diesel in twenty years."

"I'll tell him you said that."

Before we parted, Theo asked why I'd never called him. I told him I was sorry and then gave him Alec's cell number—which technically he already had—and told him to text me if he was feeling lonely. I wanted Alec to get whatever message Theo had to send me, to understand that even though I'd followed him across the country, my loyalty was not to be taken for granted.

Alec beat me home. He was watching a French movie, all accordions and lovers rushing up to one another in brick alleyways. I hated when he did this—my French was terrible and he refused to use subtitles.

I went into the kitchen, where I was determined to make a cheese soufflé. Soufflés were Alec's favorite—he would have to apologize if he wanted to eat any.

"I'm making a soufflé," I called to him. "Cheese, not chocolate."

Like clockwork, he appeared in the kitchen. "What was that stunt on campus?" he asked. "Who was that dude?"

"A friend."

"A friend? You have friends now?"

"Yes. His name is Theo and he's my friend. What about the redhead? Is she your friend?"

"She's my *student*," he said. "They're this weird thing you get when you're a *teacher*."

"I see."

"You think I'm fucking her," he said.

I looked up at him. "No, I don't. I *know* you're fucking her."

"Well, I'm not. She's my best student."

"Once upon a time, I was your best student."

This was supposed to be a joke: I'd barely done the homework in his class. One time, I turned in a receipt for a Wendy's milkshake and he handed it back to me with a bright red A+ across the top. He smiled at me, the cute smile where his green eyes went twinkle-twinkle. He may have been oafish and bald, but he was attractive in a Viking–meets–Mr. Clean sort of way.

"I'm mad at you," I said, getting the eggs from the fridge. "I don't like it here."

"I know you don't."

"So what are we going to do about it?"

He sighed, turned off the twinkle in his eyes. "What do you want to do?"

"I should probably go home, right? That would make the most sense." As soon as I said it, I knew it wasn't what I wanted. Like anyone without a backup plan, I wanted the original plan to work out.

"It's not even winter," he said half-heartedly. "Maybe you'd like the winter?"

"It doesn't even snow here. I looked it up. What kind of place doesn't snow?"

"It snows in the mountains. We can go to the mountains and see snow."

"I don't want to go see snow like it's some relic in a museum. I want it to actually snow. I want it to rain. I want the sky to do something, anything at all." I was suddenly tired. The "house" was hot, the air thick and fragrant. There were orange trees in the yard and in the evenings they let off a sweet, sickly odor.

Alec took me into his arms. He used to smell like a thunderstorm, but they didn't have the same laundry detergent here, and so now he smelled like nothing. He had always reminded me of thunderstorms, the mixture of rain and wind and power. We'd spent our first week together in bed, spring storms raging outside. During the days, I worked at the university's map library, and he'd come visit, bringing peanut butter sandwiches and sodas. We'd play the map game, in which one of us would name a town on a map and the other had thirty seconds to find it. In the evenings, we'd walk back to his apartment, where we'd watch movies and eat take-out, wait for the room to flash yellow with heat lightning.

He didn't feel the same in California. How could he be like a thunderstorm when there were no thunderstorms to compare him to? When I looked at him, it was like a layer had come off, revealing some muted version of the Alec I'd known back in Kansas. I wondered what he saw when he looked at me.

As he held me, I closed my eyes and pretended like we were back home. In the morning, we'd walk to the bakery around the corner and split an order of biscuits and gravy, share a mug of coffee. We'd go back to his apartment and make love, do a crossword, read books. I realized all of this was possible in California—there were biscuits and gravy, bakeries and crosswords. But it wouldn't be the same. It couldn't be.

"Are you tired?" he asked.

I nodded, my tears dampening his shirt. *I miss you*, I wanted to say.

"Let's go to sleep," he said. "Forget the soufflé."

We shuffled to bed, where I immediately fell asleep. At some point in the night, Alec left the bed and went to sleep on the couch—he'd done this once before, saying it was cooler there than in the bed, where I radiated heat.

In the morning, I put on a red tank top and gathered my hair into a ponytail. Wearing my hair up gave me a headache, but every time I did it Alec complimented me. *You've got such a pretty face*, he'd tell me. The morning felt sad, and I wanted to look pretty for him.

In the kitchen, he looked up from the table and squinted at me. I waited for him to compliment my hair, but instead he said, "I got a dick pic at one in the morning. Guess from who?"

I bit my lip.

He had a piece of paper in front of him, which he slowly pushed toward me.

"What's this?" I asked, although I could read what it was: a ticket from Sacramento to Wichita.

"We'll get you some big suitcases so you can check a couple bags. Everything else, I'll mail you." He looked down at the ticket, ran a hand over his head.

"Is it the girl?"

"No."

"Then what is it?"

"It's everything. It's every minute since we got here."

I was trying not to cry. "Do you still love me?" I asked.

He sighed, looked again at the ticket. "It's like every day, I'm trying to take a goldfish for a walk—nobody's really enjoying it."

A moment passed in which my body floated outside of itself, bumped against the ceiling like a helium balloon. Then he said, "I thought putting your hair up gives you a headache."

The room grew dark, a tint of gray swallowing everything it touched: the table, the walls, Alec. As quickly as it came, it left, restoring the house to a mocking brightness. Closing my eyes, I imagined my first breath of air in Kansas. It would be cold already, a layer of frost twinkling on the sidewalks. My mother would collect me from the airport in her minivan, the same old lightning bolt crack in the windshield. She would not say anything—she wouldn't have to. We would simply drive off through the saddest, ugliest city in the world, a city of Burger Kings and pawn shops and antiabortion billboards and residential streets bursting with plastic playground equipment and ratty front yards patrolled by toddlers in dirty diapers, snot dripping from their grimy little noses—noses their mothers would die to protect. Inevitably, my mother would turn to me and smile. Put a warm hand on my knee and squeeze three times. *I. Love. You.*

A Million and One Marthas

Paige invited me over so we could cook our skin cells. Laying out, she called it. It would be me, her, maybe a few of the other Preps. I wasn't a Prep, but I was on my way, slowly rising through the ranks one tube of kiwi lip gloss at a time. Only a week before, they'd cornered me after gym, eyes bright with endorphins, pastel shorts rolled down to expose a strip of golden waistline, and asked if I wanted to eat lunch with them. *Yes, yes, a thousand times yes!* I'd wanted to scream, but instead just shrugged and said, "Whatever."

The Preps sat at the Deluxe Table, named so because it was both next to a window and far enough from the lunch monitor that you could execute petty crimes, like trading cigarettes for Trojans or just saying *titty-fucker* without getting an after-school detention. I usually sat near the trash cans with a quartet of quiet girls who read fantasy novels or drew manga while eating Lean Pockets. At the Deluxe Table, the Preps shared a paper plate of prunes, sliced mangos, and rice cakes. My mom had packed me turkey and mustard on rye, which I promptly threw away, untouched, along with the yellow Post-it that read: HAVE THE BEST DAY EVER! Exactly why I'd been invited to this lunch was a mystery. Had there been some kind of meeting? Had an oracle visited Paige in her dreams? It was possible they thought I was new to school, new to Wichita—I'd just gotten contact lenses and lost fifteen pounds by eating nothing but celery sticks and Mentos— but I didn't want to think I'd been completely invisible before my transformation. Perhaps they just wanted someone to bear witness to the inner sanctums of their beauty, their coolness. Perhaps they could sense how desperate I was to be one of them.

On the day of the laying out, I made my mother drop me off a block away from Paige's house, so nobody would see the horror of her van.

"This place is pretty chichi," my mother said, looking around at the houses, the streets so wide they were called avenues. "Can you take a picture of the kitchen?"

"You're kidding."

"I'm just curious, Laney. These people. It's like they live in a television show. You'll see."

I got out of the car before she could ask me to steal a roll of toilet paper.

Paige's house, which was not really a house but a mansion, belonged in one of the catalogs my mother kept beside the toilet. The door was large and wooden and shaped like a gravestone, flanked by shrubs neatly shorn into teepees. I rang the bell and then crossed my fingers for a butler in full regalia—top hat, waistcoat, monocle—but it was Paige who eventually opened the door. She mumbled, "Hey," and then turned around, as if I was there to sell cookies.

Inside, the smell of old wood and clean emptiness—leather and lemon, everything either ancient or modern. Through gossip I knew that Paige's father made his money from some sort of high-end children's toy operation. Contrary to the whimsy of his career, there was a rusted mace above the doorway and a polar bear rug that could have easily been faux if not for its yellow teeth. Because my mother loved home decorating shows, I had seen dozens of houses like this come to life, one hired hand at a time. I could imagine the lean interior designer flying through the front hall, shouting where to put the reclaimed wood wine bar, how high to hang the Swarovski crystal chandelier, his pointed crocodile boots clicking across the sea of hardwood. All the while, Paige's father would nod in silent approval from a leather armchair, a rare Pokémon card ensconced in his breast pocket.

To think that people really lived like this. My mother's house—my house—was like a waiting room. Beige curtains. Beige couch. A glass bowl of chewable mints to keep you occupied until the gynecologist was ready to see you. My mother claimed to have once owned a small landscape portrait by a French artist named Suponte, in whose massive and continuously rising auction value she firmly believed. Who Suponte was, I couldn't say, but it didn't matter much since my father had stolen the painting when he left us—for a woman named *Kitty*, I was told. My mother nursed the story like a binky. At the end of every month she would sit at the kitchen table, bills fanned out before her, lamenting, *If only he'd left us the Suponte.*

Judging from Paige's house, it would have taken a fleet of disappointing fathers to destroy the bulk of her family's wealth. She looked natural among her father's money, as if she too had been shipped in by a designer. She fluttered through the entryway in a sheer white halter dress, her black hair up in the kind of messy bun that took hours to construct. The other Preps were drinking lemon water in the kitchen, where a heavyset woman in jeans and a floral apron was arranging cheese and crackers on a tray.

"Is that your mom?" I asked Paige.

She laughed, looked at the other Preps. "You're hilarious. My mom basically lives in Cabo."

"You girly girls hungry?" the woman asked, smiling to reveal a missing canine. You could tell she'd been pretty once, when she was a teenager. Big eyes, big lips.

"Martha, I *just* had a smoothie," Paige said. She looked back to the Preps and rolled her eyes. "Jesus. It's like she wants me to be as fat as she is."

Martha either didn't hear or pretended not to and continued arranging the snack tray. My impulse was to go over and help her— my mother had taught me never to watch someone else work—but I knew such a gesture would be suicide. Instead I laughed, sucked in my stomach.

In addition to Paige, there were three other Preps: the class sex goddess, Stephanie Pattuci, whom everyone called Sexanie, and the Farha twins, Holly and Molly, who looked like a pair of Lebanese Barbie dolls and whose mother owned a chain of popular fitness clubs. Holly and Molly were identical in every way except that Holly was kind and Molly was awful. Once, on a field trip to Exploration Place in the fifth grade, Molly put a piece of dried dog poop in my backpack so that everybody, including the beautiful, red-haired tour guide everybody wanted to impress, thought I'd pooped my pants. It used to be that Holly had a big, dangerous-looking mole above her lip, but she'd had it removed over summer break so now you had to just wait and see what kind of Farha you were dealing with.

Paige went around solemnly kissing everyone on the cheek—a new fad among the freshman girls—before leading us to the back of the house, where the perfect yard collapsed into a pool of twinkling water outfitted with floaties and a diving board and a gratuitous hot tub bubbling up into the late August heat.

"It's so fucking lame," Paige said, stripping down to an ink black bikini that revealed a tiny rhinestone stapled to her belly button. "All these stupid pool toys. It's like, who even plays in the water anyways?"

She and the other Preps took their places on the lounge chairs and began slathering themselves with baby oil. My great-aunt Janice had recently survived a nearly fatal bout of melanoma, but I happily joined them in the oiling, wondering if anyone would notice my swimsuit. I'd gotten it the night before, after begging my mother to buy me a new one. In the dressing room at JCPenney, she insisted on watching as I tried things on. "You'd be better off with a one piece," she'd said. She had an idea that I wasn't developed enough for a bikini. Obviously, she was out of her element. Not to mention a pervert. Maybe I hadn't fully developed the bust that was sure to one day be mine, but there was definitely something there, something that had to be retained by a garment with more horsepower than a girl's Speedo. In the end, we settled on a canary yellow bikini with a generous amount of padding and a scandalous bow that tied at the breastbone. At home, I shut myself in my room and practiced seduction dances. I pictured Paige going red with envy. Even she wouldn't have a swimsuit like this. "Ain't nobody got a suit like mine," I chanted as I gyrated before the mirror, ignoring the full rack of identical suits back at JCPenney, not to mention all the JCPenneys across America. "Ain't nobody, nobody, nobody."

What nobody also knew was that I had a plan to make a name for myself. This would happen by seducing Paige's older brother, Tucker, who was said to be a spitting image of a young Johnny Depp, circa *What's Eating Gilbert Grape*. The problem with Tucker was that he was homeschooled, so nobody had ever talked to him. Even Paige kept quiet on the matter of her older brother, only mentioning him once, by accident, to tell us that her father had gotten him a Jeep for his birthday, and how stupid, since Tucker never left the house. Which was true. Tucker did not go to parties or play sports or race pickups in the country with the Andover boys. Rumor held that he was a genius and that Paige's dad had shipped in a team of Russian scientists to formally train him in physics and engineering. Either he was in the process of building a rocket ship that ran on pop tabs, or he was creating a naturopathic cure for canine anxiety. He was a myth inside of a fortress, and I was determined to break through with the cannon of my burgeoning womanhood.

Once we were sufficiently oiled, I turned to Paige and sighed what I hoped was the sigh of the wearily wealthy. "It's a great house," I told her. "The décor is to die for. Who all lives here?"

Paige yawned. "Like, my family?"

"It just seems like there are a lot of rooms."

"There are a lot of rooms. It's a big house."

"It is," I said. "Enormous." My mother once told me never to buy a big house, even if I had the money. *You'll spend your whole life dusting rooms you never go in*, she said.

Paige looked over at Sexanie, and I imagined her eyes rolling behind her sunglasses. Still, I pressed on. "So who all's in your family?"

"Like, my parents and my brother? We used to have one of those cats from the cat food commercials, but it shed everywhere so my dad put it outside and it basically froze to death. What about you? Do you have any siblings?"

"I'm an only child."

She laughed and settled further into her chair. "Thought so."

I wasn't sure what this was supposed to mean, so I focused instead on my body, making sure my suit was positioned in such a way that my boobs looked big and my tummy flat. Not that it mattered; nobody was looking. But at any moment they might.

After a few minutes of idle talking, the girls went quiet so that the only sound was the sound of the pool filter gulping for air and the distant bass of a rap song on the patio speakers.

In time, I was bored and hot and longed to get in the water. It was midafternoon, the sun trained on us like an interrogation lamp. Kansas was in the thick of a heat wave; for more than a week the high temperature had hovered just below 100. Figuring the heat would knock the girls out for at least a half hour, I decided it was the best time to act.

"Is there a bathroom inside?" I asked Paige.

She squinted at me and sighed. "Only like twenty. Just go in and open doors till you find one."

I rose from my chair and walked back to the house, whose massive shadow now reached across half the pool. Glancing back, I admired the Preps lying in a row, their painted eyes shut to the sun, thin bodies glistening with future cancer. How lovely it was to be one of them.

It still seemed a dream, to be at Paige's house. She'd once flown to L.A. to be in a commercial for Crest whitening strips and on weekends her dad let her drive his extra Lexus, even though she barely had her learner's permit. I'd witnessed this only once, when she'd come in hard to the parking lot of the Warren Theater, where my mother and I had tickets to an abysmal PG feature. The other Preps threw their hands into the buggy summer air as Paige dialed up some gangster rap. One of the Farhas was smoking a cigarette that she eventually threw to the ground and twisted out with the toe of her stiletto, just like in the movies. I found it all very glamorous—a pack of fourteen-year-old girls in high heels and silver eye shadow piling out of a Lexus. My mother mumbled something about a circus car of child prostitutes.

Paige's kitchen was cool and empty. A bamboo ceiling fan whirred overhead, but otherwise the house was silent, as if it were not really a house but a dream castle constructed by Paige's imagination. I wondered where Martha had gone, if perhaps she ceased to exist when Paige no longer needed her.

I made my way to the staircase, which was wide enough to accommodate a row of von Trapp children. The second floor opened into a living room with a big flat screen TV and a row of suede couches. At the far end was a long hallway, the walls covered in gilt-framed oil paintings of men and their hunting dogs, old wooden ships teetering on the crests of frothing waves. I inspected the faded, curled signatures—none were the work of Suponte.

The door to Tucker's bedroom was not closed because there was no door—it had been removed, leaving a pair of naked hinges. Inside, Tucker was sitting cross-legged on a massive bed, surrounded by a moat of pillows. The rumors were true—he was gorgeous. At least gorgeous enough. On the Johnny Depp spectrum he was perhaps closer to *Pirates of the Caribbean* than *What's Eating Gilbert Grape*, but still. He had wide shoulders and a massive, boulderlike head. Despite his size, he operated with the jerkiness of a child, as if unaware of his proportions. He was darker than Paige, who had fair skin and a splatter of freckles. Perhaps he used a tanning bed.

The bedroom was sparse—a bookshelf filled with books, a walk-in closet filled with shirts (it, too, had no door). Like in a preschool classroom, everything came in primary colors: red, blue, yellow. A single orange baseball cap hung outlandishly from the peg of a wooden coat tree. There was no laboratory with bubbling beakers, no workbench or telescope, not even a desk. Perhaps these were somewhere else—in the basement?

"Knock, knock," I said.

He looked up, revealing a small white canvas in his lap. Beside him lay an open cigar box, inside of which sat a plastic tray of watercolors and a Ball jar of murky water. I couldn't tell what he was painting—it was a blur of colors. Blue and brown. A streak of orange.

"Who are you?" he asked. A nervousness rose up in him so quickly that the canvas shook in his lap, the mason jar rattling against the cigar box.

"I'm one of Paige's friends. My name's Laney."

This information seemed to calm him. "What are you doing up here?"

"I felt like being alone for a minute."

"Well, you're not doing a very good job, are you?" He smiled—he really was attractive. His good looks were, I now saw, afforded by his stature—all that weight and muscle, the bonus of his smile. He looked older than a high school guy—maybe early twenties. His jaw was the jaw of an adult.

"Come here," he said, and patted the spot beside him on the bed. "Sit by me for a second."

I climbed onto the bed. Sitting was not an option, as it would make my stomach bulge, so I lay down beside him. The bed was comfortable, one of those memory foam things where a lady in a nightgown can jump up and down and not disturb the recklessly placed glass of wine on the other end of the mattress. Tucker turned to me and smiled. I felt mature, as if we were great lovers on our honeymoon in Paris. I imagined his room as a château. There were violinists on the street below, or maybe on the veranda, whatever a veranda might be. A silver platter of champagne and grapes.

"Why's there no door?" I asked, suddenly aware that his father, or Paige, or anyone else could walk in at any moment.

"I got rid of it."

"Why?"

"They're ugly," he said. "Metaphorically speaking. They close people out. Separate."

I believed, then, in his genius. Moments like this, I liked to think of what my mother would have to say about me, in bed with a prodigious boy I hardly knew. Would she be amused? Impressed? Most likely, she'd be angry, but I liked to think that somewhere beyond the immediate anger she would feel humored. *That Laney*, she would think. *Always trying for new things, meeting new people.* I would live the adventurous life she'd been too afraid to live.

"Why don't you go to school?" I asked.

"Sorry, what was that?"

I repeated the question.

"Who says I don't?" And then, "Did you know that you're beautiful?"

The blood rushed to my face and I smiled so widely I feared I might look crazed or, even worse, ugly.

"Will you roll over for me?" he asked.

"I'm not a dog."

"Don't worry. I just want to give you something. A tattoo."

I rolled over and lay still while he unclasped my bikini top, his fingers grazing the skin on my back. My heart beat beneath me. Here I was, with Paige's brother. In his room. On his bed. Beautiful.

"You're completely safe," he said. "I just don't want to get paint on your suit."

"Do you like it?" I asked.

"I do. It's the perfect color for your skin."

I smiled into the bed. "What are you putting on me?"

"It's a surprise—don't try to guess. Just close your eyes."

I did as told and soon felt the wet tip of his paintbrush on my skin. The brush tickled, but I tried not to move.

"You're a good patient," he said. "Almost done."

When it was over, he blew on my back, igniting the cold paint so that goose bumps rose across my body.

"What is it?" I asked.

"You really want to know?"

I nodded.

"It's my name." He kissed the back of my neck, so softly it almost didn't happen. "Now we wait for it to dry." He then began to run his hands through my hair—something my mother sometimes did if I was feeling sad. I would lay with my head in her lap and she would stroke my head until I fell asleep. Tucker's hands were warm and strong against my neck. I wondered if he was going to try to have sex with me and, if he did, whether I would try to stop him. Part of me worried I would regret not going all the way while I had the opportunity. And yet, losing one's virginity seemed like something that should happen in a dark room, where certain body parts could not be properly seen, and that Tucker's room was too bright, too open, for anything so potentially embarrassing to take place. Another part of me was terrified. But his hands just kept on, raking my hair, digging into my skin. I wondered if perhaps he was a gentleman, if this was what people talked about when they talked about not sleeping with someone on the first date.

Eventually I asked him what time it was. Paige and the girls would be looking for me.

"Not sure," he said. "I don't think there's a clock in here."

I reclasped my top before I sat up and looked outside—the sun was still high but I couldn't be sure how much time had passed. "I have to go," I said.

"Stay."

"I can't. Maybe I'll see you later?"

"Promise me," he said, an intensity in his voice, "or I'll come find you."

"All right," I said. "Promise."

He then grabbed me and kissed me on the forehead, his lips leaving a wet circle on my skin.

"You're fascinating," he said, the pupils of his eyes widening. "Do you know that?"

All I could do was smile. Nobody had ever called me fascinating. I had always suspected I was, and yet I had also felt, deep down, that it required a man's endorsement in order to be true.

"I want you to have this," he said, and from his pocket removed a silver bracelet. I recognized it as the bracelet all of the Preps wore, a simple chain with a silver heart that read: PLEASE RETURN TO TIF-FANY & CO, NEW YORK. I'd wanted one so badly the year before that my mother had finally caved and bought me one for my birthday. Upon closer inspection it read: PLEASE RETURN TO TIMOTHY & CO, NEW JERSEY. Eventually it turned my wrist the color of an olive and a powerful rumor circulated that I was suffering from a highly contagious form of gangrene.

"Really?" I asked, knowing that this bracelet was the real deal—people like Tucker had no need for knockoffs.

"I bought it for my girlfriend but we broke up," he said. "I want you to have it now."

"Only if you really want." I gave him my wrist and sat very still as he clasped the bracelet.

"There," he said. "Looks better on you anyway."

Outside, the girls were still on the lounge chairs. They'd turned over, so their backs were to the sun.

"What took you so long?" Paige asked, perhaps insinuating I'd gone number two. She opened her eyes but did not bother to sit up.

"Nothing—I just couldn't find the bathroom right away." I was delirious with joy and bewilderment, a touch of fear. What exactly had happened with Tucker? Nothing, technically, but also something, metaphorically. I was still unsure how I would reveal my secret—how I would tell Paige and the others that I'd seduced her brother, that I'd made him fall in love with me. That I was beautiful. And *fascinating*.

"You didn't use the upstairs bathroom did you?" she asked.

"No," I said, my heart skipping a beat. "Why?"

"Just wondering. It doesn't have a door."

"Why not?" one of the Farhas asked.

"It's my brother's bathroom."

"But why no door?" Sexanie asked.

There was a pause. I wanted to say, *Because he's brilliant and lovely and wants to share himself with the world*, but Paige spoke first. "It's my dad's idea of a punishment. He caught Tucker doing coke again, so his big idea was to get rid of his doors. As if there aren't a thousand other doors in the house." She looked back to me and then, removing her sunglasses, narrowed her eyes onto my wrist. "What's that?" she asked, gesturing to my hand.

I put my arm down against my side. "What's what?"

"Your wrist. Let me see your wrist."

I had no other choice. I held out my hand.

"Where'd you get this?"

"Nowhere. I've had it."

"No, you haven't. I lost this a week ago—it was in my purse and then it was gone."

"I didn't take it, if that's what you're thinking." Sexanie and the Farha twins were now eyeing me, as if they'd known all along that it would come to this.

"So it just, what? Walked out of my bag and crawled around your stupid wrist?"

"Actually, your brother gave it to me," I said, a feeling of power rising inside me. Knowing I had to give it back, I unclasped the bracelet from my wrist—my *stupid* wrist—and then set it on the chair next to Paige. I then sat very still, waiting for something to happen. *You did* what *with my brother?* Paige would ask. The other girls would gasp, a shocked admiration in their eyes.

"That's weird," Paige said, "because my brother's in rehab."

A feeling of dark unease settled over me. "He's what?"

"I said he's in rehab. In Oklahoma City."

"Then, who's the guy?" I knew I shouldn't have said it but I did—there was no escaping it.

"What *guy*?"

"There was a guy," I said, knowing I'd already entered dangerous territory. "Upstairs."

"You *just* said you didn't go upstairs."

"I guess I was there for a second."

"And you're saying there was a guy up there?"

I nodded. "I thought he was your brother."

"No fucking way," Paige said.

"Who was it?" I asked. My stomach was starting to turn. Sweat ran down my back, where the paint was.

"Did he have, like, a gigantic head?"

I nodded—it was true, now that she said it out loud. His head really was gigantic.

"Dennis, Martha's son. He used to come with her on weekends, so he could watch our cable and eat our food or whatever, but he's not allowed in the house anymore. My dad caught him stealing some of

Tucker's clothes. So fucking gross. Like, get your own undershirts for Christ's sake. It's not like we're paying Martha in potatoes."

I thought of Tucker's fingers in my hair—were they really Dennis's fingers? And so what if they were? I didn't want it to matter, but of course it did. A wave of nausea shot through me.

"So Dennis just gave you my bracelet? Or did you have to suck him off for it?"

"I didn't do anything," I said, although now it felt like I had.

"Right," said one of the Farhas. "Because boys just give out jewelry."

"Whatever," Paige said. "Guess it's time to fire Martha."

"What do you mean? It was just him. She wasn't even there—"

"Laney. There's a million and one Marthas in the world. Get over it."

I wondered, then, how many Paiges there were. How many Laneys. Meanwhile, Paige had pulled out her cell phone and was punching in numbers. "Who are you calling?" I asked.

"Oh, just my father." She smiled wickedly and then, with the hand not holding the phone, dangled the bracelet in front of me. "Hey, you really want this?" she asked. With a flick of her wrist, she tossed it into the pool. She mouthed the words: *Go fetch.*

I wanted to say something, anything, but I couldn't find the words. My skin was buzzing. I could think only of the name on my back, the paint now dry and tight across my skin. Without warning, I got up and dove into the water. It was the exact temperature water should be. Cool, but not too cool. Warm, but not too warm. Manufactured for the optimal comfort of Paige and her family. I began clawing at the skin on my back, rubbing away the paint. When I opened my eyes, the water around me spun ribbons of red, then green, then black. It was just paint. Just a name. Just a boy in a room in a house that wasn't mine. Below me, the bracelet made a squiggle against the floor of the pool. *Fuck it*, I thought, and swam hard toward the bottom.

Go On, Eat Your Heart Out

Patty stepped on the scale and the red needle arced forward: 188 pounds. How had this happened? How, to use Bryan's words, had she *let* this happen? She assessed her nude profile in the bathroom mirror. *Great White Whale*, she thought. Was this even a real species of whale? Shark, sure. But whale?

"Patty, are you almost done in there?" It was her younger brother, Kurt.

"Just a second," she said, and then grabbed her towel—meant for the beach, with cartoon martini glasses and conch shells—and covered her body. Living with Kurt was like being transported to their mother's house, circa 1997. Back were the rituals of their adolescence: the endless up and down of the toilet seat, bickering over who deserved the last Oreo or whether to watch *Cops* or *The Simpsons*. Adding to the awkwardness was Kurt's new girlfriend, Madeline. She was young—too young for Kurt, in Patty's opinion—and seemed to subsist primarily on carrots and Swiss chard, foods that belonged to a larger category of semiedible fodder known as "clean foods." The whole thing screamed eugenics to Patty, but she could never tell this to Madeline, who worked at one of those primeval gyms where people transported artificial boulders from point A to B or took sledgehammers to truck tires. More than once, Patty had come home to Madeline and Kurt making out on the living room sofa, Madeline's lemon yellow JanSport fanny pack still fastened to her waist.

Patty opened the bathroom door to find that Kurt and Madeline were also in towels. Patty hated when they showered together, not only because she had to endure the audio, but also because it was one of the many small pleasures Bryan had denied her, along with foot massages, sleeping past ten o'clock, and eating food in bed. He said he never felt clean after sharing a shower, and that afterward he'd just have to shower all over again, by himself, which would be wasteful. Feeling self-conscious, Patty hoisted her towel but something went haywire and it came loose, revealing the entirety of her right breast.

"Good God," Kurt said, clapping a hand over his eyes. "Are you trying to blind us?" He hurried into the bathroom, Madeline trailing behind him.

After the door slammed, Patty could hear Madeline saying, "You didn't have to be so mean. She's your sister."

"Am I not letting her live here for free? She's six years older than me, for fuck's sake."

This had become Patty's life: a stampede of embarrassment. There was the rhinoceros of breaking her chair in the middle of a poetry reading, the gazelle of sweating through her white blouse on the walk to the post office. Ugliness would have been better. To be ugly was to be a victim of poor fortune, while to be fat was to advertise a failure of willpower. A failure of strength. Patty had only recently learned this, although it was something she had suspected all along, perhaps since she was a little girl and the kids at school had made fun of the obese lunch monitor, Miss Audrey. When it was time to wipe down the tables, nobody wanted to touch the washrags, which, according to third-grade folklore, were made from Miss Audrey's soiled underwear.

Safe in Kurt's computer den, which served as her makeshift bedroom, she hugged her pillow. It was technically Bryan's pillow, but he'd let her keep it, most likely because it smelled like the prescription-strength deodorant she'd started using the summer before. Bryan hated the deodorant. He said it smelled like steel wool, although the fragrance advertised was spring showers.

No more crying, she told herself. Bryan had never liked crying. On the occasion she failed to hold back tears in his company—and there had been many of these occasions, before he kicked her out—he would look away, as if to give her privacy. She was allowed to pee in front of him, but crying was not tolerated.

She blew her nose and then went to the computer to look for jobs, a task that more often than not devolved into a marathon of YouTube videos. Slam poetry was her latest obsession. Here were women even younger than her—twenty-two, sixteen, seven—rhyming about global warming and bulimia and, in the case of the seven year old, why every little girl deserved a pet giraffe. Kurt's computer chair creaked beneath her as she scooted toward the desk. She had one new e-mail, from Bryan. Her heart quickened. "Hi, Patty. You left your blender here. Do you want it? If not, I will use it. Take care. —Bryan Marconi."

His last name! And take care? The room closed around her, making her keenly aware of the space she occupied. She could feel her belly cascading before her. Where was her belly button, even? It seemed the very source of her life had disappeared inside her.

Of course it had come to this. A last name, a blender. She had never deserved Bryan, who ran ultramarathons and was the highest paid app programmer at CellCo. Bryan, with his curly hair and that god-damned dimple that materialized when he shaved his beard. Bryan, who'd once been asked to model boxer briefs for Sears.

Patty used to be beautiful, too. At her thinnest, in college, she was 109 pounds, nearly a whole fourth-grader less than she was now. Her delicate nose and short, feathery hair had given her a gamine look that she cherished, sometimes turning and smiling in front of the mirror for so long she'd be late to class. She did not take this body for granted. She ran five miles every morning—a warm-up run for Bryan—down to the community lake and back, so that on weekends she could slip more easily into silky dresses and go dancing in the Power and Light District with her friends—most of whom now had long since married and moved away from Kansas, closer to mountains or water.

That was all before she met Bryan—while trying on running shoes at REI—before she fell into him like a helpless child down a well, going and going through all that cool darkness without recognition or panic. It was also before she caught him downtown, on the five-year anniversary of their first date, eating gelato and playing a serious game of footsie with the mousy waitress who worked mornings at their favorite brunch spot, Café Bonita. Annette was her name, as if even her parents knew she would grow up and trap other people's boyfriends. This was before Patty forgave Bryan once, and then again, and then a third time, all the while nursing her aching heart with cheese cubes and crusty baguettes and bar after bar of Peruvian dark chocolate. Instead of her usual breakfast of espresso and ice water, she took to eating stacks of French toast or glazed donuts, buttered bagels and cranberry muffins the size of softballs. She would find sugar underneath her nails. Crumbs in her bra. Meanwhile, she began sleepwalking. She would wake in the kitchen with a hand full of croutons, peanut butter in her hair.

Aside from losing Bryan, giving up her clothes had been the worst. Who knew that they mattered so much? Before, nothing looked bad on her. Once, after polishing a set of her mother's silverware, she'd forgotten to take a salmon-colored terrycloth rag out of the back pocket of her jeans. Afterward, while walking downtown, she overheard someone say, "I read about that in *Vogue* the other day. Terrycloth is so *in*." Now she found herself forced into plus sizes, the tags reading 2x and 3x to avoid the suggestion of pornography: xxx. Depressing. All of it was depressing.

It was June now and she'd been living with Kurt for nearly a month, not wanting to commit to a place of her own, lest Bryan change his mind and invite her back. She missed their house in Westport. It was, after all, the one *she* had demanded after many aggravating weeks of house hunting. Lots of light and built-ins, a little reading nook and a swinging porch out back by the garden. Not too far from the grocery store or the library. But he was right: he could afford the mortgage, she could not. She had lost her job at the radio station when she could no longer stop crying on the air. What money she had was Bryan's, given to her out of the kindness of his heart. He did not want to see her struggle. To see her struggle would hurt him. She understood that the real purpose of the money was to alleviate his guilt.

Now, what to do about the blender?

"Dear Bryan," she wrote. "I would like the blender back, but I'm out of town for a while." This was true, or true enough. Kurt lived in Lawrence, a good hour away from Kansas City. Plus, "out of town" created the illusion of vacation, of tropical climates and European vistas. "As I may not be in KC any time soon, why don't you hold onto it for me, and I can come get it the next time I'm in the area? This might not be for some time—maybe around the holidays. Thank you. Patty Graber."

The holidays could mean anything between Thanksgiving and New Year's. The summer was just gearing up, which meant she had a good six months to diet. *Starting today*, she told herself. And then, remembering the German chocolate cake in the refrigerator, decided that tomorrow would work just as well.

As she eased into her diet, Patty thought often of what Bryan told her when she first found Annette's muddy flip-flops in the back of his Volvo. "She has an energy," he'd said. "When I look at her, I feel hopeful." "And what do you feel when you look at me?" Patty had asked, her heart funneling deeper and deeper down the drain of her body. Bryan had refused to answer the question. All he could say was that he was sorry. That it wouldn't happen again.

The whole thing made little sense. Sure, Annette was young and thin, but she was not particularly pretty. She had oily skin and split ends that broke off and littered her white serving apron. Her nostrils were covered in tiny red veins that gave her the appearance of always having a cold. But it was true she had an energy about her—a glow even Patty couldn't refute. Annette whistled as she served and always drew something playful on her copy of the receipt—a smiling banana, an octopus shaking a pair of maracas. She was exciting, something Patty worried she herself had never been. Bryan had sometimes poked fun at her for it—how she had a hard time finding the appeal in things like sledding or cruises or concerts. She liked quiet pleasures that required little risk: reading mystery novels, watching movies, eating ice cream with hot fudge. Even in her party days, she'd only tolerated the clubs because she had an idea she might find a boy-friend there. Really, she hated everything about going out—the loud music, the crowds, waking up in the morning with her ears ringing, her hair smelling of cigarettes. How stupid, in the end, to have met Bryan while shoe shopping. All those wasted mornings spent hungover. But Bryan loved going out. Loved drinking. Meeting strangers. Dancing. Annette surely liked dancing, too—she had the body for it, long and lean with a ballerina's figure.

Patty was pleased when slowly but surely the weight left her, sloughing off like layers of skin. By late August, she weighed 166 pounds but had not yet found a job. Bryan was still transferring her money every other week, but the number grew smaller and smaller. "I hope you're enjoying your vacation," he wrote in an e-mail. She didn't bother to respond.

Meanwhile, Kurt and Madeline were still together, paused somewhere on the timeline between lust and calamity. Kurt's relationships always ended poorly: he was handsome enough to afford it. He liked to keep women at a distance, so that he could more easily discard them when he found one he liked better. But Madeline seemed different. She was always around the apartment, which she kept tidy and infused with mint-rosemary room spray. She was the kind of girl who stored bulk food in mason jars and drank fermented tea—the kind of girl Patty had always found slightly irritating. And yet, slowly but surely, Madeline had grown on her. She was smarter and funnier than Kurt's other girlfriends. One afternoon, she'd gone around the apartment and glued a tiny pair of butt cheeks over every photograph of Kurt's face. Kurt had kept the butt cheeks up for a week before finally taking them down. Even then, he did not throw them away but put them in a pile by the microwave.

Madeline knew about Patty's diet and had, on several occasions, shown up at her door with offerings of coconut kale smoothies or chalky, sugar-free protein muffins. Once, she walked in on Patty watching YouTube videos and the two spent the rest of the afternoon in front of the computer, swapping their favorite clips. Patty showed

Madeline her favorite slam poets and Madeline showed her videos of people performing superhuman feats: a guy climbing Half Dome without a rope, a woman deadlifting a baby elephant.

"How do people get this way?" Patty asked.

"Years and years of hard work," Madeline said. "You know, you should try coming to the gym one day. We can do a workout together."

"I can barely change a water cooler."

Madeline waved a dismissive hand. "You don't have to be strong to work out. That's the whole point—it's about building your body from the ground up. About tapping into your core potential."

Patty figured she'd give it a shot. If nothing else, it would make Madeline happy.

The gym was called Hard Core Fitness and was essentially an old warehouse outfitted with dumbbells and blue gymnastic mats. In the back, a man who looked like Mr. Clean was carrying a pair of paint buckets up a metal staircase that led to nowhere.

"The buckets are filled with concrete," Madeline explained. "We call it muscle painting."

"That guy's arms are bigger than my head."

"That's the end goal. Muscle burns calories even when you're not exercising. Did you know that?"

Patty did not. She stood half-admiring, half-despising Mr. Clean as he carried out his Sisyphean task. It seemed unfair that men were given permission to grow unchecked while women were expected to dwindle down to their smallest possible form.

They started with a series of floor exercises: squats, push-ups, lunges. Madeline held Patty's feet so that she could do sit-ups. They were about to start lifting when Patty noticed a trio of men at the front door, all of them dressed in basketball shorts and white V-necks.

"Oh, shit," Patty said.

"What's wrong?" Madeline asked. "Are you feeling sick?"

"It's my ex."

Madeline looked toward the door, where the men were collecting towels and water bottles. "Do you need to talk to him?"

"I'd rather not. We're not supposed to see each other until . . ."

"Until what?"

"Until I'm ready to. Would you mind if we left?"

"But we just got here."

"I know. But if he sees me I might combust."

Madeline sighed. "All right. Grab your stuff."

They managed to sneak out while Bryan and his friends were in the locker room. In the car, Patty apologized. "We can come back another time. Maybe during the day, when I know he'll be at work?" Madeline agreed, but Patty could tell she was disappointed. "I'm really sorry—I know you've been wanting to show me the gym."

"It's not about me or the gym," Madeline said. "It's about getting you out of the house. You sit around all day reading and sucking on ice cubes. It can't be good for your mind. Or your body."

Patty wanted to explain everything—how she'd told Bryan she was on vacation, how she didn't want him to see her until she was thin. But she couldn't tell Madeline any of this without revealing how pathetic she was. "I know," Patty said. "It's just hard."

"People do hard things every day," Madeline said.

"Is it possible I'm just not one of them?"

"It is," Madeline said, her tone serious, "but only if you keep thinking that way."

Later that week, at dinner, Madeline told Patty about a job. A friend of hers managed the used bookstore downtown and was looking for someone to work a few weekday shifts.

Patty shrugged. "I guess I could do that." She was drinking her nightly vanilla-flavored protein shake, slowly sipping it through a straw so as to savor it. For dessert, she would eat exactly fourteen purple grapes.

"Don't sound so excited," Kurt said.

"I am excited," Patty said. "Or at least I'm trying to be. It's just hard."

"Why does it have to be hard? You love reading. Madeline wants to help you get a job at a bookstore. Why's it so hard to be excited about that?"

"You don't understand," Patty said. "You've never been sad. You're too good looking."

"Oh, come on," Kurt said, rolling his eyes. Patty could tell part of him was flattered.

Madeline put her fork down. "I get it, Patty," she said. "You're in a rut. But I think this job will be a good thing."

They ate the rest of the meal in silence, Madeline and Kurt sawing at their chicken, Patty taking careful sips of her shake, her stomach growling as she steadily filled it. For some reason, she liked that Madeline had chosen the word *rut*. It was a thing with three parts—a beginning, a middle, and an end. For the moment, Patty was inside of the rut, but all she had to do was work hard enough, and she would eventually come out on the other side.

The bookstore was a good thing in that food was not allowed inside. Everything was paper and ink, the air heavy with the musk of old books. She mostly worked alone, which afforded her time to read when there were no customers. She began with a romance novel in which a handsome Swedish rock star made quick work of seducing a plain Jane elementary school principal. Then came a brief stint with P. G. Wodehouse. Then, finally, the cookbooks.

She'd never understood cookbooks. Why spend the money when you could find recipes online? But when she opened the first one—a tome on vegetarian cooking—she suddenly understood the fuss. The books were made by people who cared deeply about food. Every recipe came with a glossy photograph and a detailed description of the tastes and textures, the ideal situation in which to eat food x, y, or z. She read about how to make the best breads and pastas, the sweetest jams and puddings. How to poach the perfect egg for avocado eggs Benedict and fry a block of savory ginger-soy marinated tofu. In time, she found that the words replaced her hunger. Once, when she was certain that nobody was in the store, she pressed her tongue to a recipe titled "Aunt Rochelle's Apple Cinnamon Spice Cake with Decadent Caramel Buttermilk Frosting," so certain was she that she would taste the capital A's crisp tartness, the warm, sugary sponginess of the word *cake*.

Occasionally, Madeline would stop by with an iced coffee and the two would riffle through the incoming books, looking for inscriptions. "Dear Kathleen," one of them would read out loud to the other, "I hope this book brings you as much wisdom as it brought me. Here's to years of friendship!!! —Elizabeth." The book would be titled something like *A Woman's Guide to a Life without Men*. Madeline also understood when not to laugh. Like when they found, "I know we haven't talked in a few years, but I'm always here when you need me. —Dad," scribbled inside the cover of *Chicken Soup for the Cancer Survivor's Soul*.

Patty liked the company and always dreaded the moment when Madeline would look at her watch and say she should probably get going. Patty hated to see her leave. Every day, when she came back to Kurt's apartment, it was a relief to see Madeline's messenger bag on the coat hook, her hemp loafers in the hall. She hoped Kurt would not fuck things up.

Who knew the hardest month would be November, with its pumpkin-spiced everything and bowls of leftover Halloween chocolates popping up everywhere, including the lobby of Madeline's gym, where Patty now took a biweekly Zumba class?

To her relief, it seemed the diet would be over soon. She had lost nearly all of the weight. When she stepped on the scale, the red arrow arched lazily up to 135 and then stopped. The change had affected her mind as much as her body. She'd begun to think of food as something distasteful—an enemy out to destroy her. Sometimes she would pass a display case of pastries and think: *You want to kill me.* She preferred her food in print.

Now, when she looked in the mirror, she was happily surprised by what she found there. All along, she'd been a Russian nesting doll: multiple versions of herself tucked neatly one inside the other. She imagined the extremes: an itsy-bitsy Patty, no bigger than a comma, and then a monstrous Patty blimp, its bloated hips and breasts pressing against the edges of outer space.

She liked to imagine Bryan's reaction, could picture him lifting her off her feet and twirling her in circles, like in the movies. She would be wearing ballet flats and a floral dress that buttoned down the front, revealing a hint of cleavage. She'd actually bought a dress just like this, at a boutique downtown, and was waiting for the middle button to stay fastened. Only ten more pounds. Ten more pounds, and she would be happy—the dress would fit, the diet could end. The problem was that she seemed to have hit a wall. Every morning, no matter how little she ate or how far she'd run the day before, the scale produced the same number: 135. 135. It wasn't a terrible number, but 125 would be so much better, so much more comfortable. Just ten more pounds and she could message Bryan about the blender. Thank god for the blender. She wasn't even sure if it was hers—she couldn't remember buying it.

Then it was December and everything was dead: the trees gave up their leaves, the sky turned the color of ash. She had always loved winters with Bryan, who had been raised on Wonder Bread and Coca-Cola and viewed Christmas as a perk of American capitalism. He wanted all of it: twinkle lights, mistletoe, the frightening animatronic Santa Claus from Walgreens that moaned "Ho Ho Ho!" when you pressed a button on his hat. Of course, this year would be different. Any festivities would be left up to Patty. Kurt was agnostic, more out of laziness than conviction, and Madeline was Jewish.

Patty decided she would get a Christmas tree, to make the apartment less depressing. She found a handsaw and an ax in Kurt's tool closet and went out into the living room, to put on her snow boots. Madeline and Kurt were sitting on the sofa, glaring at one another. Patty had heard them arguing but they stopped talking as soon as she walked in. Madeline's cheeks were flushed. There were tears in her eyes.

Patty tried to be quick about the boots.

"What's with the saw?" Madeline asked, her voice shaky.

"I'm getting a Christmas tree. Just something small."

"Not happening," Kurt said. "The needles make my nose itch."

"I think it's a great idea," Madeline said, although Patty could see in her eyes that she didn't care about the tree either way. "Mind if I come with?"

Patty tried to gauge Kurt's reaction, but he was staring at his own hands. "Sure," Patty said. "If you want to."

Madeline hurried from the living room to change.

"Everything all right?" Patty asked Kurt. She was nervous, thinking maybe they had been fighting about her. Every day, she felt more and more certain he was ready to kick her out. It was clear she was starting to annoy him. He kept leaving Post-it notes around the house: "TURN THE COFFEE POT OFF WHEN YOU'RE DONE USING IT." "CLEAN YOUR HAIR FROM THE SHOWER DRAIN, THANK YOU."

He didn't answer. Eventually he looked up at her and said, "The first time I sneeze that tree is out of here."

Patty went where she always went to get a tree: a plot of land outside the city, in a town called Vinland. So what if the land belonged to Bryan's great-uncle Greg, who had inherited it from Bryan's grandfather? Bryan wouldn't know, and his uncle Greg certainly wouldn't find out. He taught economics at the University of Arkansas and came to Kansas only a couple times a year, to visit family and make sure the land was still there. Bryan and Patty had gone there often, to take walks and have picnics and, once a year, to steal a Christmas tree.

"I haven't been here since last Christmas," Patty explained to Madeline. "Funny to think how different everything was then."

They left the car, Patty carrying the gloves and hand saw, Madeline taking the small ax. The plan was to find something of manageable size that could fit in the back of Patty's 4Runner—a baby tree, sacrificed in its youth. As they walked into the woods, Patty focused on the rumbling in the pit of her gut; she'd gone without her usual breakfast of apple slices and fat-free yogurt. She was going to be extra good, to shed the final ten pounds before the new year. "Tell me something happy," Patty said. "It'd be nice to hear something happy." She wanted to ask about Kurt but was afraid of hearing something she wouldn't like.

"I guess I have happy news," Madeline said. "I got into med school. In San Diego."

Patty felt suddenly lightheaded. This she had not expected. "I didn't know you even applied."

"I didn't want to tell anyone, in case I didn't get in. I'm sorry—it seems silly now."

"No, it's not silly." Patty wanted to cry, but instead she said, "Congratulations. What kind of medicine?"

"It's a naturopathic medical program, so it's all about how to help the body naturally heal on its own. There's an entire course on herbal remedies."

"It perfect for you. Really." She did not want to say what she was really thinking: *Everyone I like has left me. Everyone is doing well but me.* "So where does Kurt play into all of this?"

Madeline stared at the ground as they walked. "I was going to invite him to come with, but I think he's cheating on me. He won't admit to it, but I saw some texts from a girl. And there was a hair tie in his car." She looked up at Patty. "He tried to tell me it was yours, but I know you never wear your hair up. It seems paranoid, I know."

"It's not paranoid at all." Of course Kurt would ruin things with Madeline. Of course he would take away the one person Patty was truly beginning to love.

"You know, you could move to San Diego, too," Madeline was saying. "There's no winter there. You could throw your boots away."

"Oh, I couldn't do that," Patty said, although the invitation made her burn with happiness.

"Why not? What's keeping you here? Everyone leaves Kansas, eventually."

Patty did not like this kind of question, and so she did not answer. She just kept walking, following the clouds of her breath. A moment of silence passed as they trudged up the hill, their feet slipping in the sludge. Kurt had disappointed Madeline, and now so had she. Perhaps it was in their blood, this capacity for disappointing others. Maybe this is what Bryan meant when he said that Annette gave him hope—that Patty had given him the opposite. That when he looked at her, he felt like he was looking at a pool of quicksand.

Just as these thoughts were opening inside her, blooming as a field of ghostly moonflowers—the seeds of which had been there all along, underfoot—who should walk up in the distance, his hand inside the hand of another woman? Bryan wore corduroy pants and the scratchy red Pendleton coat she'd given him for his thirtieth birthday. Annette wore a pair of overalls and a floppy brown ski hat with a neon pink puffball on top. It was the kind of outfit a child would wear, but Annette still looked like a young girl—gangly limbs, round face, big eyes—and so could get away with childish wardrobe choices.

"Fuck," Patty said.

"What's he doing here?" Madeline asked.

"It's sort of his land."

Madeline smiled. "I see. And who's the girl?"

"His girlfriend, I guess." Despite everything, Patty hadn't expected them to actually stay together. From what Bryan had told her, Annette had a serious boyfriend, a paramedic whom she planned to marry. Their affair was just that—an affair. But now, here she was. Her hand in Bryan's hand. Her cheeks flushed from the cold. Of course. Patty should have known.

Madeline was at her side, her hand on Patty's arm. "What do you want to do?" she asked, a bit too loudly, so that Annette turned around and faced them. *Uh oh*, mouthed Annette. Her lips were painted red.

Madeline grabbed Patty by the hand and the two walked quickly back to the car. Part of Patty wanted to stay—didn't she at least deserve a Christmas tree?—but she trusted Madeline to guide her.

"I'm sorry that happened," Madeline said. She had taken the driver's seat—she was the kind of girl who knew what to do in a crisis. Patty felt a pang of sadness, that Kurt had ruined things with her.

"It's all right," Patty said. "I should have known better." She rested her forehead against the window. She could see Bryan coming up over the hill. He was alone.

"I think he wants to talk to you," Madeline said.

"I don't want to talk to him."

"Should we leave?"

"Probably."

"Where should we go?"

Patty watched Bryan scramble down the snowy hillside. He was probably getting snow in his shoes. Good. Let his feet get wet.

"I'm pretty hungry," Patty said. "Maybe we could grab something to eat?"

Madeline started up the car. "Anything you're craving?"

It was a good question; the right question. "Ice cream? Or maybe something with cheese?"

By this point, Bryan was waving his hands, signaling for them to stop. "Patty," he was shouting. "Patty, wait a second."

Patty rolled down her window, the cool air whirling into the car. "What do you want?" she asked. The car was still moving, but Madeline slowed just slightly, so that Bryan had to jog to keep up. He looked good, jogging. An easy stride, despite the snow. Patty wondered if her face looked thin.

"I want to talk," he called.

"You have Annette for that."

"Patty, if you'd just listen to me—"

"Listen to this," she said, her voice rising. She let a moment of suspense build, her heart pounding. "You can keep the blasted blender," she finally said, and then rolled the window back up, her hands shaking. *Blasted*—where had that come from? Britain? She didn't care— she liked the way it sounded, something small exploding into the shape of a mushroom cloud. She closed her eyes as Madeline drove, going faster now.

"He said he cheated on me because he needed someone who was full of life," she said, "as if I wasn't *alive* enough for him."

Madeline glanced over, then back to the road. "I think it's good you're not with him anymore."

"Sometimes I think so, too. But mostly I don't." She closed her eyes, felt her stomach growl again.

"What was it you liked about him?"

The question startled Patty—perhaps she had feared all along that someone might ask her, that she would be forced to account for the years she'd spent with someone who could so quickly discard her. "I hate to say this," she said, "but I think I liked that he chose me."

"That makes me very sad," said Madeline.

"Me too," Patty said, realizing it was the truth. She wondered, for the first time, if the real source of her sadness was not the loss of Bryan but that she had tried so hard—was *still* trying—to make him love her. All those months of dieting and for what? He would never love her again. "Do you ever wish you could just eat and eat forever," she asked Madeline, "without gaining any weight?"

Madeline was quiet for a moment. "You know, my mom has this saying, that there are two kinds of people in the world: those who eat to live, and those who live to eat. I think I'm the first kind."

"You do *like* food though, right?"

"Of course. Are there people who don't?"

"I think there must be varying degrees." Patty turned back to the window. She felt calm for the first time in months. "What's your favorite food?"

Madeline was silent for a moment, but then said, "I guess I have a weird thing for baked potatoes, even though they're basically giant starch bombs."

"What else? Keep going. I think I need to just sit here and listen."

Without hesitation, Madeline kept on. "I love donuts—just plain glazed ones. And gummy bears. And really buttery biscuits."

Patty let everything wash over her—the sound of the names of the foods, the heat, the motion of the car as it rolled away from the trees, from Bryan and Annette and Annette's perfect figure. She found herself thinking about her old body, the fat one. A sense of mourning came over her, for losing it. She had been fat, yes, but she had also been *more*. More body, more human, more life. Why didn't everyone want to be big? To demand more of the physical world? She suddenly wished that Madeline was big, too, that they were both so big they couldn't fit in the car. That they were two hundred, three hundred, four hundred pounds. That they were as big and happy as clouds.

"I also really like sushi, although I'm sure it's better where the fish is fresh."

Patty sat still and repeated the words in her head: *Fish is fresh. Fish is fresh.* Like the sound of the ocean itself. She willed her stomach to growl. She would eat until she felt ill, she decided, and then she would eat some more.

The House on Alabama Street

When Jill was done dumping Cliff—for reasons he still did not understand—she went on a walk so that he could pack his things in peace. Packing did not take long—he had not brought much to Kansas—and so he soon found himself in the sanctuary of his busted '97 Subaru, the only place in the world that belonged only to him. No matter that the interior stank of french fries and gasoline and that one of the wiper blades was missing. Cliff made the best of it. When it rained, he imagined his windshield was waving hello. At some point, Jill had stuck a Garfield sticker onto the glove compartment. Cliff hated Garfield.

He wasn't sure where to go but he knew he had to go somewhere and so he simply drove. Without really meaning to, he started in the direction that Jill had gone walking. She must have made a turn somewhere, but he didn't feel like trying to guess where—that would be stalking—and so he kept straight.

Six blocks later, he saw the ROOM AVAILABLE sign in the yard of a house with pink shutters. Because he did not know what else to do, and because he was tired from packing under emotional duress, he decided it was as good a place as any. He looked to see what street he was on: Alabama.

The muddy doormat read STAY FOR AWHILE. To his right, a porcelain rabbit stood next to an empty terra cotta planter. A glass birdfeeder hung from the awning—when he looked closer, he saw that it was filled with spider webs. He rang the bell and counted to two-Mississippi before a woman appeared. She was slender, with hair that seemed devoid of color, like a fingernail. Freckled breastbone, too much brown eye shadow, gold bangles. She could have been anything between thirty-five and sixty.

"I'm here about the room," he told her.

She looked him up and down. "You a Harvard boy? My husband was a Harvard boy."

He remembered his T-shirt, which read HARVARD ROWING TEAM. "Not exactly," he said. "I'm from Connecticut. Picked this up at a thrift store."

"Connecticut," she said, as if it were a new word. "What brought you to Kansas? School?"

"A girl, actually," he said. It seemed, now, like a stupid reason.

"It's either school, a job, or a girl," she said. "Or death. Those are the only reasons for coming to Kansas. Unless you're born here, of course. Then it's a matter of escaping." She smiled, letting Cliff know this was a joke.

Cliff wanted to disagree, to find some more romantic view of the plains, but the truth was that he knew nothing about the area except that you couldn't buy liquor at the grocery store and that the governor was something of a madman. "It's not a bad place," he said. "The people seem nice." He hoped this would make the woman like him. He often worried that women did not like him.

"It's the trade off," she said. "No mountains or water but people will look you in the eye."

He nodded, suddenly self-conscious of whether he'd been making eye contact.

"Well, let's get you inside. Seems there's a lot to talk about."

Based on the exterior, Cliff expected cross-stitches and doilies, stale potpourri and cat litter, but the kitchen had chrome appliances and marble counters and the air smelled like hazelnut coffee. Through a bay window he could see that the backyard was large and well kept, with wicker patio furniture and a garden bed. In the living room, a set of tasteful blue throw pillows were arranged just so. It could have been his mother's house. Or Jill's.

Cliff was nervous. He knew it was an interview, but it seemed more for the sake of a nice time than anything else. She brought out a plate of ginger cookies and two glasses of milk. She told him her name was Adelheid DeLuca, but she would prefer if he called her Heidi.

"I'm Clifford, like the big red dog," he told her, "but you can call me Cliff."

This made her smile. She was prettier when she smiled. "So what's the news about this girl?"

"It's a long story," Cliff said, although he worried maybe it wasn't—that it was, in actuality, a fairly simple tale of love undone by location.

"That's all right," Heidi said. "I like stories."

He found it a relief to tell someone, to hand over the story as if each part were a weight in a bag he hadn't realized he was carrying. As he talked, Heidi ate cookies and twirled the fringe of a woven placemat. He could tell it had been a while since anyone had told her a story.

His went like this.

He had met Jill four months before, at a lodge in Yellowstone where he'd been working as a bartender. Because she was in college, Jill had come late in the season and had a plan to leave early, before her classes started. New employees brought fresh air to the lodge, which, to those who had been there since April, had grown suffocating in its remoteness. Like all newbies, Jill was immune to the tourists and the frustrations of communal living. She was still in awe of Yellowstone and would, many times per day, make time to watch Old Faithful hiccup into the sky. She came to the lodge like Noah's dove, bearing proof that the world outside the park was still alive and well. She had stories about her life in college, about professors and exams and the reprieve of house parties. She still craved Chinese food and movie theaters, luxuries Cliff had learned to live without.

Because Jill worked housekeeping, she smelled, in his bed, like lavender fabric softener. Eventually, his happiness took the shape of a ticking bomb. From the moment of her arrival, he began to prepare for the blow of her departure. On her last night, he readied himself for the sadness that would unfold come morning, but it was during these final teary hours that Jill had invited Cliff to join her in Kansas once his contract was over. "I have extra room in my closet. You can park for free on the street." Together, they would live as a normal couple in the real world, far from the bubble of seasonal work.

When his contract ended in October, he made the long and mostly flat drive to Kansas only to be dumped ten days later. "You're just not the kind of guy I want to date here," Jill had explained. At the park, he'd been popular and interesting—he rock climbed and could identify edible plants and had, on more than one occasion, returned to Jill's room with a grocery bag of fresh huckleberries— but in Kansas, he was just another average-looking, uneducated freeloader. Nobody cared that he had once climbed the Grand Teton with a broken thumb, or that he'd helped a ranger chase down a man who threw a bag of Doritos into a thermal pool. Here, his history counted for nothing. He had no friends. He was not in school. He was no one.

He could feel it in himself, too. He was an entirely different person in Kansas than he'd been in Yellowstone, just as he was an entirely different person in Yellowstone than he'd been in Connecticut, where he'd finished high school with a B average and spent two mind-numbing years watering plants at his dad's nursery while taking classes at the juco. What this meant about him as a person he could not say, but he knew it wasn't good. He did not want to be the type of man whose appeal depended on location or circumstance.

Heidi hummed and nodded. "It's a sad story, but I'm mostly concerned about your education. You never finished undergrad?"

"I'm dyslexic," Cliff explained, hurt that she didn't care about his broken heart. "The readings got too hard. And seasonal work was fun. I'm a good bartender—I can talk to people."

"Oh, phooey," she said, grabbing for another cookie. "Reading's just one way of getting at information. But I see what you mean." She took a bite of her cookie, crumbs falling into her lap. "I can help you, if you'd like."

"Help me?"

"If you live here, I can help you get started at the university in the winter. My husband was a professor, so I'm familiar with the system.

We can get you some financial aid, maybe some grants. Most important, I can help you with your readings. It'd be good for me. I'm out of my mind with boredom, with my husband gone."

Cliff considered the idea. He could go back to school, where he would become the type of person Jill wanted. The type of person who belonged in a town like this one. He could feel a sense of hope rising inside him. All along, his ticket back to Jill—back to a life he could be excited about—had been just a few stop signs away, on a street named after a state he'd never been to. What did he know about Alabama? Nothing. There was a possibility he could not locate it on a map.

"I guess we could try it out," he said.

Heidi smiled. "A new chapter for you. A new chapter for me."

A week passed, then two. Cliff hadn't seen Jill, but this wasn't a bad thing. He wanted to be better before he saw her—enrolled in classes for the coming winter, ready for school.

Most mornings, he and Heidi converged in the kitchen for breakfast. She would stare dreamily out the window as she stirred molasses into her oatmeal, a daily ritual Cliff had come to anticipate, as certain as the sunrise or the steam whistle blowing from the university, which sat on top of the town's largest hill. He would spread peanut butter on toast, drink coffee, and scan the paper for a better job. He'd picked up a couple shifts at an Italian restaurant downtown, but he didn't much like it. His clothes perpetually stank of marinara sauce, and one of the dishwashers, a townie named Rico, kept finding surreptitious ways to touch Cliff's butt.

"How's the room working out?" Heidi asked one morning. Students could be heard outside, walking or biking to class. They seemed, always, to be shouting.

"The room's fine," he told her. "Everything's fine."

She looked relieved. "You wouldn't believe how many people turned it down. I tried everything. Added hard wood. Changed the curtains. And the paint. I changed the paint a few times and still nobody took it."

"I'm not sure why. It's a good room."

"Well," she said, smiling to herself. "I'm glad you like it."

The room was, in fact, perfectly fine. It had everything Cliff needed: a queen bed and a modest desk where he'd stashed the few postcards Jill had sent him during the short time when she'd been in school and he at the lodge. The curtains did look new. They were a dark blue, made of a thick, silky material that kept the light out in the morning.

Cliff wondered if it was not the room but Heidi herself that had kept tenants away. There was something unsettling about her—a kind of puppy dog eagerness that made him feel that she might, at any moment, set herself in his lap and demand to be petted. In the mornings, she refilled his coffee without his asking, as if she was his waitress. At night, like clockwork, she appeared at his door with a cup of chamomile tea. When he finally admitted to not liking tea, she arrived with hot cocoa and thin lemon cookies that melted on his tongue. The problem was not the coffee or the cookies, but the conversations they inspired. She would ask him questions—How was his day? Was he liking Kansas? Had he tried any of the pie she left in the fridge?—and so long as there was a mug in his hand, he was obligated to answer.

"You know, your room used to be my husband's study," Heidi was saying. "He'd hole up in there for days, writing and writing, and then sneak out at night, like a little mouse, to steal food from the kitchen. That was how he had to write his books—he said it was the only way. Total isolation. This was back when our son was in the house. You can imagine how it made him feel."

She had never mentioned a son, and there were no pictures in the house, of a husband or anyone else. Only landscape portraits and a variety of mirrors and clocks. "I didn't know you had a son," Cliff said.

"That's his room across from yours. I keep it locked. But it's there for him when he visits." Her mouth turned down in a way that suggested to Cliff that her son did not often visit. "It wasn't as bad as you'd think. Sometimes people, especially people who love one another, need space so that they can miss each other. A certain degree of loneliness can be critical to a marriage."

Cliff wanted to ask what had happened to her husband but was worried she might cry and that he would be expected to consol her. He stared into his coffee and tried not to think of Jill, which was, in the end, just another way to think of her. He had work in the afternoon and then a dinner date with a girl named Sandy who was a line cook at the restaurant. Dating coworkers was strictly forbidden, but Cliff felt the misdemeanor was owed to him. He saw it as a chance not for romance but as a way to get out and do something in this town, which was a sleepy, uninviting place if you weren't affiliated with the university. He also had a secret hope that he would bump into Jill. Sandy was a junior in the school's journalism program and was bound to have large circles of friends. He was taking her to dinner and a show at a bar downtown, a bar that Jill had once mentioned to him.

"When should I expect you home tonight?" Heidi asked.

Cliff stood and placed his cup in the sink, not wanting to meet her gaze. He suspected she wanted to make him dinner.

"I'm not sure," he said. "Probably late."

Work was fine and the date was fine. Sandy was, in every way, average, if not a touch irritating. All through dinner, she kept asking Cliff if she had food in her teeth. He thought of Jill, of the endearing gap between her front teeth. Later that night, when he noticed a piece of spinach pasted to the surface of Sandy's front tooth, he said nothing.

The only interesting part of the date was during the walk to the bar, when Sandy tripped over a stone in the middle of the sidewalk. The stone was situated on top of a metal manhole cover, along with four other rocks of different sizes and shapes. "God damn these things," Sandy said, rubbing her toe. When Cliff asked what they were, she explained that every Sunday for the past few months, a woman had gone around placing exactly five stones on every manhole cover in the downtown area. He'd wanted her to explain more, for this little story to open up a trap door that would lead to other interesting stories about the town and the people in it, but Sandy said this was all she knew—how was anybody supposed to know why a crazy lady did crazy things?—and requested that they stop at a drug store so she could put antibacterial ointment on her big toe, which had begun to bleed, but only slightly.

Eventually they'd gone to the bar, where she'd admitted to not knowing anybody. She claimed it wasn't her usual place and then refused to dance to the band, which was too indie for her taste. The end of the night featured a perfunctory kiss that stirred nothing but loneliness in Cliff. It was not like kissing Jill, which conjured a primal sensation from somewhere behind his belly button. Sometimes, when he thought of Jill, this spot still ached; he imagined it glowing a fantastic white if put under an X-ray.

Because he did not wish to extend the date beyond the show at the bar, Cliff arrived back to Heidi's house at a reasonable hour. She was still awake, reading beneath the light of a gaudy brass lamp. At some point she'd told Cliff a story about the lamp—some long anecdote that took place in a foreign country and involved an act of cultural savvy on her husband's part—but he could not, at the moment, remember the details or why the lamp was at all important.

"Cliff," she called out. "Come in here and tell me about your date."

He considered walking straight to his room, pretending not to hear her, but a sense of guilt guided him into the living room, where he sat down on the sofa across from her. He noticed that while he'd been gone she'd dyed her hair, which she usually wore in a single braid down her back but which, tonight, she'd let down, so that it fell across both of her shoulders. The color was meant to be black, but looked purple in the light of the lamp.

"How did you know I was on a date?" he asked.

"Oh, I can always tell with boys. It's so obvious. The cologne. Your nerves."

He allowed himself a smile, amused that he'd been so easy to see through. "The date was fine. Nothing special."

"Not the one?"

"Definitely not."

She took a piece of her purple hair and twirled it around her finger. "Ask me how I met my husband."

Cliff did not want to ask, but knew that he had to. He hoped the story would not take long. "How did you meet him?"

She sat up straight, as if invigorated. "He saved my life in the Grand Canyon. I was hiking with a friend and we had stopped to have a snack. Grant and a buddy of his were hiking up as we were hiking down. They stopped and ate with us and we ended up chatting. That's when a bee landed on my knee. You should know I'm deathly allergic to bees—my throat closes right up. I tried to stay calm but I had a whole scenario built up in my head—helicopters and one of those horrible stretchers that dangle in the air. That's when Grant just flicked the bee right off my leg, like you'd flick a fly from a piece of fruit. He went right on talking as if nothing had happened, but I'd decided he'd saved my life. We met up again at our campsite that night. And that was that. No dates about it."

Cliff could not decide what to say. A nearly identical situation had happened to him and Jill. She'd been eating a turkey sandwich and he'd flicked a wasp from her wrist. She'd had tears in her eyes—she said she always got teary when she saw wasps—and then told him he'd saved her life. He'd brushed it off as mere dramatics, but from that moment on they were inseparable. She would come visit him at the bar, where he'd give her cups of maraschino cherries, whose stems she claimed to knot with her tongue, but which she really tied under the bar when nobody was looking. Occasionally, he'd pocket one of the knots so he could find it later and make himself smile. He'd found one just the other day, at the bottom of his laundry basket.

"Is it a good story?" Heidi was asking. "Some people think it's silly. They don't see the point. It's not that I was in any real danger. Most likely the bee would have flow away. The point is that when two people are meant for one another, these little things—the bees—they become fate. The universe plants them around us, and it's our responsibility to notice them."

Cliff was suddenly uneasy. She had just articulated the thing he'd been trying to resolve in his mind since meeting Jill—the very magic that had kept him from moving on from her, from moving away from

Kansas. He felt there was something larger than him or Jill or their relationship at stake. The universe had willed them together—what were the chances of a boy from Connecticut meeting a girl from Kansas in Yellowstone?—and their breakup was an act of defiance against it. If the world handed you an oyster, weren't you at least obligated to search for the pearl? There were other, more peripheral superstitions: that his lucky number was seven and Jill was the seventh girl he'd ever slept with; that all of the best people in his life—his grandmother, Lynn; his father, Carl; his best friends, Jay, Saul, and June—all had one-syllable names; that he and Jill had both, at different times, owned a cat named Bubbles.

"I think it's my bedtime," Heidi said, and placed her book facedown on the coffee table. She looked at Cliff with a carefulness that made his heart ache. It was as if she understood what had happened between him and Jill and was apologizing for it. "I'm so happy the room worked out," she said. "It's a relief to have a man in the house again." She immediately said, "Oh, I didn't mean it like that. Not like you're replacing anyone—"

"It's fine," Cliff said.

"But I want you to know," she went on, "if you ever need anything—" She shrugged. "I don't lock my door at night. That's all I wanted to tell you. I don't lock my door."

"Heidi," he said, suddenly embarrassed for the both of them. "I don't think—"

"I forgot to tell you I'm a little drunk. I should have said that from the beginning—I've had some wine. Don't listen to me. Okay? I'm just drunk." She smiled at Cliff, but he could see she was humiliated. She turned and headed toward her room, where he knew she would cry, having made a fool of herself. She had once mentioned to him that she did not drink; her mother had been an alcoholic.

At the sound of her door closing, Cliff let out a breath. He sat for a moment as the house hummed around him. How had he ended up here, in this strange house in the middle of Kansas? He wondered what Jill was doing at that very moment. Drinking a cocktail? Taking a shower? Kissing another man? Eventually he couldn't stand the living room, with the ugly brass lamp and the blue throw pillows. He went to Heidi's door and knocked.

"Come in if you really want to," she said.

Hers was the master bedroom, but aside from the walk-in closet it was no bigger than his own. There was a girlish quality about it—the wallpaper was lined with red and white roses, and Heidi lay on a light pink comforter with what appeared to be a stuffed penguin behind her head.

"Are you upset?" he asked.

"I'm just embarrassed. I'm always embarrassed around you."

"You shouldn't be."

"Why not? You're a young man and I'm a disgusting old woman."

"You're not disgusting," Cliff said. "And you're not so old."

Blue makeup was running down her face, collecting in the wrinkles under her eyes.

Cliff came closer to the bed, with an idea of consoling her. It was then he saw the reusable shopping bag, filled to the top with stones.

"They're rocks," Heidi said, noticing him looking. "My husband and I would collect them everywhere we went. Free souvenirs."

"You put them outside," he said. "On the sidewalks."

Heidi turned over, so that her back was facing him. "Let's just go to bed now," she said. "I'm so tired. You can stay here, if you want. I'd like that. But don't do anything you don't want to. I'm not about to be accused of forcing anyone to do anything they don't want to."

Cliff stared at the rocks. The thought of sleeping with someone—anyone—was appealing, and yet he knew what a single night of intimacy could do to two lonely people. At the lodge, it was not uncommon to wake up in the bed of a friend, unsure of how you'd gotten there but relieved that you had.

Cliff knew he should turn off the light and shut the door, leave Heidi alone in her bed. But he found himself undressing. Not completely, just down to his boxers and undershirt. He climbed into the bed and put an arm around Heidi. A loose hold, but there he was, his weight around her. The mattress was soft with age and they sank toward the center.

"Nothing else will happen," he said. "Only this."

She said nothing, but pressed herself into him. He did not press back, but he did not move away, either. She kept pressing but in time gave up. Her body went limp and she began to snore.

Somewhere between this and sleep, he decided it was time to see Jill.

The streets in town were named after states, in order of when they'd been admitted to the union. It seemed a betrayal to Cliff, as if the town's residents secretly dreamed of living somewhere other than Kansas, a desolate state filled with desolate people.

Jill lived on Tennessee Street, in an old green house with white trim. There was a big front porch where they had, during their few days together, eaten cereal from ceramic mugs and watched people make the hungover pilgrimage home. Since he'd last been to the house, someone had set up a hammock. An unfamiliar cactus stood guard beside the front door.

Before he could knock, Jill opened the door and did a double take. "Cliff. I was expecting someone else."

Cliff cleared his throat and tried to figure what to do with his hands. "I wanted to see you," he said. "Can we talk?"

"I'm sort of expecting someone—"

"Can we get coffee later then? Or dinner?"

She frowned, and he knew then that all of the doors he'd once passed through to get to her were locked and would never be unlocked again. "Are you still living here?" she asked.

Cliff nodded, not stopping to consider that this confession should embarrass him.

"I figured you would have moved somewhere else. Back to Wyoming. Or back home."

"Well, I didn't. I'm here."

"Where are you living?"

"I'm renting a room, from the wife of a professor. Or at least they used to be married. I'm not exactly sure what happened to him. It's just down Twelfth, on Alabama."

Jill frowned. "The last name's not DeLuca is it?"

"Do you know her? She's been really great to me. She's offered to help me with school—with my reading. That's what I wanted to tell you. I'm going to enroll in classes. I want to get my degree."

"Cliff," she said, frowning.

"What? What's wrong?"

"Everyone knows her. Her husband—the professor—he killed himself. He tried to kill one of his students."

For a moment, Cliff thought she was trying to be funny. "What do you mean? When?"

"Just last spring. He was a big name, was supposed to give a million speeches for graduation. Apparently he'd been having an affair with a student and when she cut it off he couldn't handle it. He had a plan to kill her, but I guess when he got to her house he couldn't do it. Said he loved her too much. That's when he went home and shot himself." She looked at him, perhaps to see if it was a good story. "His wife never mentioned it, before you moved in?"

"No," he said. "I assumed they were divorced. Or that he had a heart attack or something."

She looked at him as if to say, *Of course you would think that.* "Everyone says she's kind of nuts now. I mean, who would stay in a house like that? I'd have been out of there the same day."

There was a pause in which Cliff felt he should say something to defend Heidi, but he couldn't figure what. That she was old? Nice? His friend?

"You know, it's kind of funny," Jill was saying. "The guy I was dating last year used to have a thing with the girl—DeLuca's student—and when he found out about everything, about how she was almost murdered, he basically fell back in love with her. I was like, fuck that. So I started applying for jobs. That's how I ended up in Yellowstone."

Cliff didn't know what to say. He remembered Jill talking about an ex-boyfriend. She hadn't said much about him, only that he had broken her heart, that he was good at tennis.

Behind him, a car was pulling up to the house. Cliff turned to see a man get out of the car. He was tall, with a beard and reflective sunglasses. He wore a chambray shirt and leather boots—he could have been anyone in town.

Cliff looked back to Jill, who was trying to keep from smiling. She bit her lip and looked from the man back to Cliff, and then back to the man.

"Jill," Cliff said.

"I told you," she said, speaking through her teeth so that the other man would not hear. "I told you I was expecting someone."

To his relief, Heidi was not home. Cliff went straight to his bedroom, where he sat on the bed and reconsidered the room in light of the new information: the curtains, the hard wood, the paint. He wondered if remodeling had been painful for Heidi, or whether it had afforded her a kind of liberation, to erase the most intimate part of her husband's life—the place where he had lived and written, the place where he had hidden from her. The place where Cliff now hid from her.

He did not know what to do with himself, in the sense of the short term or the long term. He did not like his job or the town and he did not, at the moment, like himself. And what about Heidi? And the room? And school? He tried to figure what it meant for him, what his next move should be. He thought about researching the dead professor but then decided against it. He wondered if he should apply to another seasonal job, somewhere he'd never been. Maybe Big Bend? He knew people who worked there; the housing and food were not good, but the weather was mild. There would not be snow.

Heidi returned home and broke his train of thought. "Cliff?" she called. "You home?"

Cliff held his breath, unsure whether to answer. "Yes," he finally said, and came out into the hall where he saw her standing with a black-and-white kitten in her arms.

"I found her on my way home from the library. Isn't she sweet?" She petted the cat and then placed it on the ground, where it sniffed her shoe before making its way down the hall, cautiously, toward Cliff.

Cliff lifted the kitten. He saw that it had fleas, along with a rather painful looking bald patch behind its ear. "Heidi," he said, holding out the cat. "It's got fleas. Maybe you should keep it outside until you can take it to the vet?"

"But she'll run away. And I want to keep her."

"She's sick, you can see it."

"I'll take her to the vet on Monday."

"But the fleas will spread—I don't want to deal with fleas in my room."

"You'll leave soon anyway, so it won't matter." Heidi took the cat from Cliff and went into the kitchen, where she used her free hand to fill a bowl with half-and-half.

Cliff followed after, alarmed that she had read his thoughts. "What's that supposed to mean?"

"I'm not as dumb as you might think. I can tell you don't like it here."

"That's not true," Cliff said. "But, while we're on the subject, there are some things you haven't told me."

"What have I not told you?"

"About your husband."

"And what does my husband have to do with anything?"

"Well," Cliff began. "He killed himself."

Heidi's eyes, usually tired, were now awake with anger. "Has it been a problem, that he killed himself? Has it somehow affected your life-style here?"

"He lived in my room," Cliff said.

"Well, he certainly doesn't anymore."

He could tell he was upsetting her. He didn't want to, but he kept on. He had a point to make. "It's just something I would have liked to know upfront. So I could have understood your situation."

"And what is my situation?"

"You're mourning," he said. "You're a widow and you're in mourning."

"A widow," she said, as if testing the word, how it felt on her tongue. "I'm a widow. Well, that explains everything." She bent down and petted the kitten, which was now lapping up the cream. "Actually, what does that explain?" She stood again and faced him. "What does that mean—that I'm a widow? Am I a leper now? Are you worried I'll infect you? That the *house* will infect you?"

"You wanted me to sleep with you," he said, embarrassed to say it out loud.

"It was a mistake, and I'm sorry if it made you uncomfortable. I can promise it won't happen again."

They looked at each other, acknowledging how far their conversation had strayed. "The thing is, I'm quite lonely myself," Cliff said. He did not mean to say it, but there it was.

There was a pause, in which Heidi allowed herself a smile. The smile seemed both miraculous and ominous, like the resurrection of something dead—a postmortem twitch of muscle. Then, without warning, the smile was gone, and Heidi put her face into her hands. She crumpled to the floor, startling the cat so that it pounced from the kitchen and out of sight.

Cliff stooped down and put his arm around her, making sure he did not squeeze so tightly that his intentions would be misconstrued. She was shaking. He did not want to be there but he was. He did not want to hold her but he did.

"Please don't leave me," she said, her voice soft. "Will you stay? Just for the year? I need noise in the house. That's all. You don't have to talk to me. I just want to know that you're here. That somebody's here. That somebody . . ." She could not finish her sentence. She was heaving now, trying to catch her breath.

Cliff felt his entire body stiffen. He did not want to hurt her, to be the kind of man who made promises he did not plan to keep. And so he said nothing.

Night of Indulgences

In the light of the hotel lobby, Ben admired his prostitute's dress. It was short and simple, with eyelets along the bottom hem—the kind of dress a young girl might wear to church on Easter morning. Because it was the night before Easter, Ben couldn't decide whether the dress paid homage to the holiday or spat in the face of it. He liked the dress and figured it must be expensive. Designer clothes were always this way—plain, boring, less about the effect than the craftsmanship. Ben knew this was how some people ended up spending a hundred dollars on a polo shirt. He had, in fact, just bought himself a coat of this caliber. Why there even existed a coat like this in Wichita, where people happily sported Nike tracksuits and terrycloth rompers, he had no idea—but Ben considered it an investment. Good things happened to men who wore coats like this one. It was made of Italian camel hair and had a row of horn buttons smooth as wishing stones. What sold him was the lining, a cream silk interrupted by stripes of ballet slipper pink. He would soon move to Virginia to start law school in the fall, and although he'd been told autumns in Charlottesville were mild, he couldn't help but picture himself wearing the coat as a series of white-haired professors approached him after class, admiration twinkling in their eyes.

Earlier that night, Ben's best friend, Freddy, had admired the coat. "That *coat*," was all Freddy could find to say. "A coat of coats."

They were having espressos at their usual starting place: a Parisian-themed coffee house where they had both, at different points, had sex with the blond barista who worked weekends. Like always, Freddy folded a twenty-dollar bill into a little origami butterfly and left it as the barista's tip. True to tradition, she pretended not to see it.

They came to this café as they had every spring for the past five years, to caffeinate before spending a careless amount of money on food, alcohol, and cigars. Afterward, they would seek some form of physical or moral destruction: taking a chain saw to a pair of old Macintosh computers or dropping gallons of milk from the roof of a Hyatt parking garage, laughing as the jugs detonated around passersby below. Once, they snuck into a frat party at Wichita State and posed as Bill Clinton's nephews. They'd come prepared, with doctored photos of them and Bill fly-fishing in Arkansas. After racking up free booze, they'd stormed through the sleeping porch, pocketing whatever they could find: iPods, watches, half-crushed protein bars. They then urinated onto a row of boat shoes before running as fast as they could, both of them drenched in sweat and shaking from what had felt, at the time, like a nearly fatal combination of freedom and adrenaline.

They'd come up with a name for these nights, used first in jest but eventually in earnest, like all the worst nicknames. They called it the Night of Indulgences. Ben marked the day on his calendar and knew that Freddy kept a countdown and could say, at any point in the year, how many days until the next Night.

Each year, the boys made a point to push their extravagance a little further—an older whiskey, a rarer cigar. This year, Ben was determined to have the best Night of Indulgences yet, as he knew it would likely be his last. A law student was expected to have a sense of propriety. Plus, he would be on the other side of the country—an expensive flight, a commitment of time. He didn't mind giving up this tradition in exchange for the rich life that awaited him—a life that had the potential to be even greater than Freddy's.

"How'd you afford it?" Freddy was asking, of the coat.

"It was a gift," Ben said. "From my father." This was a half-truth. While his father had given him a modest sum of money with which to do whatever he pleased—fun money, he called it—it was assumed to be what Ben would live off of for the first few months of school. Rent was not cheap out east, and Ben hadn't saved much at his part-time job at the *Wichita Eagle*. He was taking out a massive student loan to cover the cost of tuition.

"I really got it for the lining," Ben said, and opened the coat so Freddy could admire the sensitive interior.

"I've never understood the point of a nice lining. What's the fuss if nobody can see it?"

"I take it you're also against lingerie?"

"Who says I don't get to see lingerie? Remember that one?" Freddy gestured toward the barista. "Wore a little red thing. Like a shoelace."

The boys laughed, all the while trying to catch the angry eye of the barista, who had, at some point, pocketed the twenty-dollar butterfly.

Their next stop was dinner, where they ordered bloody steaks, monkfish liver pate, and a bottle of honey-colored bourbon aged for longer than either of them had been alive, all served by a waiter with an unidentifiable accent. Ben thought the restaurant must have hired the man because of this accent; to people in Wichita, there was nothing more sophisticated than something, or someone, from a foreign country—the right foreign country.

When the meal was finished and Freddy had paid, the two moved to the balcony to smoke cigars. Ben thought back to when they were boys and Freddy had stolen one of his father's cigars for them to smoke after school. When the time came, Freddy said his asthma was acting up, and so he simply watched on as Ben coughed so hard that a blood vessel burst in one of his eyes—the joke around school was that Ben's eye had gotten its period. In high school, Freddy went on to make a little film based on the event. To everyone's surprise, the film won first place in a contest, forever setting the course of Freddy's future. Freddy was all set to move to Hollywood, where he had yet to find work but had locked down an apartment with a Jacuzzi bathtub and a terrace that existed for the sole purpose of drinking outdoors. Ben couldn't help but compare it to the one bedroom that awaited him in Virginia, which had no dishwasher and no washing machine and was actually just a room in a house. Ben's father taught eighth-grade science and his mother had quit selling insurance when she fell ill the winter before—the fun money had come from his father's retirement fund. Freddy's father, on the other hand, was a heart surgeon in the same hospital where both Ben and Freddy were born. The two met in Hebrew school, where they had quickly established a relationship based on a simple but sturdy arithmetic: Freddy would spoil Ben, and Ben would reciprocate with loyalty and admiration. It had begun with a remote-controlled helicopter and had progressed into their adulthood, where it took the form of, among other things, an iPad and a pair of gold cufflinks. Ben had never worn the cufflinks—he didn't yet own a suit—but kept them in a velvet box for the day he would need them.

When they finished their cigars, Freddy took out his cell phone and dialed a number. "I've a surprise for us," he said. "You go wait out front."

Ben did as he was told, nervous for what the surprise might be. The year before, Freddy had bought them both diamond earrings. Neither boy had piercings, and so, after four consecutive shots of tequila, they'd stumbled into a parlor in downtown Wichita so that a girl with an electric pink bob could slide a needle through each of their earlobes. Ben hoped Freddy had planned something more docile this year; the earring had devastated his mother.

Eventually Freddy brought his car around and honked. There were two girls, one in the front seat and one in the back. They smelled of mint gum and expensive perfume.

"What do you think?" Freddy asked.

Ben gave a surreptitious thumbs-up, pleased that the night involved women. If there was one thing he had over Freddy, it was looks. Freddy was redheaded and heavyset and had chicken pox scars on his cheeks; Ben had the look of a Kennedy—square jaw, good hair, boyish smile. Once, while shopping at the Kansas City Plaza, Freddy had held a shirt to Ben's chest to see how it looked. "Christ, I'd kill for a chin like yours," he'd said. Perhaps he hadn't meant to say it out loud because even the skin on his arms turned pink before he'd hurried off to buy the shirt. Neither of them ever mentioned the moment, although Freddy wore the shirt often.

The girl in the backseat introduced herself as Samantha. She had long brown hair and a birthmark shaped like a top hat on her shoulder. The one in the front was blond and was smoking a clove cigarette. Ben wanted to tell her how bad they were for her lungs, but when she turned to look at him, he saw she was not the type of girl who would care what he had to say. Overall, she was not unpretty. She had large, rectangular teeth that made Ben think of carrots, but her nose was the right size, and there was something comforting about her lips.

"My name's Ben," he said to her, and held out his hand.

She took his hand in the way dainty women and old ladies shake hands: by the fingers only, as if receiving a wad of money. "You can call me Claire or Anita. Betty Crocker. Doesn't matter." She let go of his hand and adjusted the hem of her white dress. The sight of her legs coming together beneath her hand ignited a set of reactions in Ben's mind. He had not, before this, understood that her purpose was to have sex with him. Even the act of shaking her hand now seemed like the opening scene of a porno. He tried not to think of his girlfriend, Alana—he'd been meaning to break up with her anyway. There was nothing exactly wrong with Alana—in fact, he'd grown quite attached to her—but she was not the type of girl he would want to settle down with. She did not own a pair of high heels and had never, to his memory, worn lipstick. There would be parties in law school, parties that demanded certain attire and an appreciation of opulence. She was the type to take a book into a spare room and sulk among the coats until the party was over. Even Freddy was too much for her—she said he reminded her of Donald Trump and that he'd once made a pass at her, although Freddy had vehemently denied doing anything of the sort. He didn't like Alana either. He called her a prude and a Catholic.

"Maybe we should all grab a drink," Ben said, hoping to stall whatever was about to come.

"Unnecessary," Freddy said. "I've got us rooms."

The hotel was busy, even for a Saturday night. It was a nice hotel, the kind with chandeliers and bellboys. The girls kept adjusting their dresses and wiping the makeup from under their eyes. Ben put his hands in his pockets and tried to feign a look of disinterest as they joined the check-in line.

"I can't stand hotels when I'm drunk," the girl said. She was standing close to him, so that her arm brushed against his. "The lighting makes everyone look like a clown. Reminds me of Vegas, in a bad way."

"Oh, me too," Ben said, although he had never been to Vegas.

"It's a nice coat," the girl said, and began to finger one of the buttons. "My dad once had a coat like this. Got it in Egypt or somewhere like that."

"How extremely interesting," Ben said, and then, when she wasn't looking, he snuck away to the restrooms. Outside the door to the men's room, an old woman was grappling with the drinking fountain. She had to stand on the tips of her orthopedic shoes in order to reach the spigot. When she was done drinking, she turned from the fountain only to knock over her bag, whose contents spilled onto the floor. *Geriatric piñata*, Ben thought. Among the mess was a crusted tube of ointment, a troubling number of sugar packets, and a toothbrush whose bristles frayed out like an ancient broom. An orange prescription bottle rolled to Ben's feet. He picked it up and brought it to the woman, who was struggling to get down to the level of the purse.

"Let me help," Ben said, gathering her things.

"Oh, you don't have to do that," the woman began, but by this point the job was already done.

"Do you want the toothbrush back?" he asked. "The bristles touched the ground."

The woman frowned. "Go ahead and put it in. And the sugars. I guess this is my punishment for pilfering them in the first place."

"Everybody steals sugar," Ben said, hoping she did not feel embarrassed. He handed her the purse, which she hauled onto her shoulder as if it were filled with sand. She thanked him, and he went to join the others in line, forgoing the bathroom altogether. He hoped Freddy and the girls had witnessed his little moment of heroics, but Freddy was in business with the hotel clerk and the girls were turned toward each other, deep in chatter. They jolted into character when they saw him.

"Where'd you go?" his girl asked, pressing a hand to his chest. "I thought you'd abandoned me."

"Just the bathroom," Ben said. He looked back and saw that the old woman was smiling at him. He smiled back at her, hoping he did not look like the type of man who was about to do whatever it was he was about to do.

Like the girl's white dress, the room was minimal in a modern way. Everything was ordinary except for the bed, which was a king. The bed excited Ben—he'd never slept in anything larger than a queen. Beside it was a mirror that reached from floor to ceiling, so that people making love could glance over and watch themselves. Ben thought about this mirror, how behind it was the room where Freddy had taken Samantha.

His own girl was busy inspecting the desk in the corner. Ben watched as she opened a drawer, removed a pen, and placed it in her little opalescent bag. It was the kind of behavior Alana frowned upon—the taking advantage of anyone or anything, including corporations—but which she would sometimes engage in with a criminal frivolity. One time she nearly died of the giggles while pocketing a bottle of Tabasco from an Applebee's. Sitting on the bed, Ben found that he missed her. He was used to being with her at night and would have liked to have her there if only to hear her opinion of the situation. If nothing else, she would have appreciated the subtleties of the night: the Muzak version of "Rich Girl" that played in the elevator, the chintzy fleur-de-lis night-light, the bowl of pastel jelly beans at the reception desk. He hated himself for missing her—for wanting milk when he'd been served champagne. They would be brushing their teeth and Alana would say something like, *Don't you love how, even when you think a tube of toothpaste is gone, if you just squeeze it hard enough you can get another week out of it?* and then she would look at him, hoping for a lengthy dialogue about the economy of toiletries. *But, Alana,* she would want him to ask, *what happens* after *that week, when you think the toothpaste is* really *gone?* It was the sort of thing someone like Freddy would never understand. Wealth made people colorblind to certain pleasures.

The girl noticed Ben sitting on the bed and took this as her cue. She sat down beside him and kicked her feet out, one by one, like a little girl bored in church. "You should know that it's my first time," she said.

"Excuse me?"

"This," she said, gesturing around the hotel room. "It's my first time."

"You don't mean you're a virgin."

"Oh, God no," she said, and laughed. "I mean my first time for money. I don't want to use the *p* word. I don't think that's what's going on here. Do you?"

Ben wanted to ask how it was any different, but he realized he also did not want to think of it in those terms. "Of course it's not the same thing," he said. "You're obviously a nice person. A *good* person."

"I don't mean that exactly," she said.

"What do you mean?"

"I mean it's not like I was advertising. Walking the streets or whatever. Freddy approached me. He asked and I said yes. He's actually doing me a sort of favor."

"You knew him before?"

She was looking at her feet, which she held out into the air before her. Little flecks of pink nail polish remained on her big toes only. "Our parents used to play tennis together." She looked at Ben, to see if he understood. "My parents won't give me anything because I had a little incident in school—so now I'm on my own. I don't have any job experience, so it's been hard finding anything that pays decent. Right now I'm at a smoothie place. I can't buy the shampoo I like. I can't eat the food I'm used to. It's been hard for me—do you understand?"

Ben nodded and thought: *My prostitute is a snob.*

"So how does this work?" She let her legs drop down beside the bed. "Do you make a move or do I?"

His heart quickened and suddenly he was warm. He realized he should take off his coat, lest he sweat through his shirt and onto the lining. As he did, the girl took off her shoes and pulled her hair into a ponytail, revealing a pair of big pink ears covered in tiny hoop earrings. He wanted to know if the jewelry bothered her when she slept, but it was not the type of thing one asked a girl like her.

"Do you mind if I turn the lights off?" she asked, but stood up to go to the switch before he could answer. It was on her way to the switch that Ben noticed the stain on her dress.

"Your dress," he said, and then wasn't sure how to politely put it.

"What about it?" She looked down and inspected her front.

"I think you may have, you know—" he motioned toward her, and it was then that she understood she was to consider the back of her dress, where a red stain had formed. *Japanese flag*, Ben thought, but he didn't dare say it.

Her face took on a look of quiet horror. She headed quickly to the bathroom.

"It's all right," Ben called to her, hoping she wasn't embarrassed. He certainly wasn't. If anything, he was relieved.

"No, it's not all right," she said. "This is my second-favorite dress and it's ruined."

He heard the water running as he sat on the bed, wondering what a man was supposed to do in a situation like this. He was relieved when she called him into the bathroom. He opened the door and found her sitting on the toilet, wrapped in a towel. Her white dress was soaking in the sink, whose water had turned a faint rose color. He'd seen this before, in his mother's bathroom when he was a teenager. It made him queasy, but he also found it somewhat endearing. Such an old-fashioned way to clean a stain.

"Can you wring it out and put it on the balcony?" she asked. Her tone was not one of embarrassment, but of frustration—a little girl's voice.

"It won't dry by the morning," he said.

"Who said I was staying until the morning?"

Now it was Ben who felt embarrassed. "Well, it definitely won't dry by the time you want to leave."

"It'll dry *enough*."

Ben gave in and drained the water from the sink, trying to hide his squeamishness. He wrung out the dress as best he could, noticing there was still a faint pink stain. He then carried it to the balcony, where he set it across the banister. He wondered, suddenly, what it would look like if it fell. He often had these sorts of fantasies—random impulses to know simply: what if? What if he were to suddenly throw his drink in the face of the waitress? What if he were to suddenly ruffle the hair of the young boy in line at Walgreens? Without really meaning to, he nudged the dress and watched as it quietly fell the nine stories down to the sidewalk below, where a drunken couple happened to be passing. The drunken man, astonished, watched as the dress landed on the ground before him. To the amusement of his girlfriend, or wife, or whatever she was, he grabbed the dress and held it up. "It's wet!" the man cried. The two looked up and waved to Ben, who waved back. Then, with the dress flapping behind them, they ran to the end of the block in a fit of laughter.

Ben kicked the balcony's metal railing and then went back into the room.

"What happened?" the girl said. "You look like something happened."

"I messed up," he said. "The dress fell."

"What do you mean it fell? Did you drop it?"

"Of course I didn't drop it. It slipped off the balcony. And then some drunk people found it."

She looked around helplessly, as if she'd just been told she had ten minutes to live. "What am I supposed to do now?"

Ben thought about the room, about what they had. "We could wrap you in a sheet and stuff you into a cab."

She gave him an incredulous look. "I'm not getting *stuffed* into anything."

"What about your friend? Maybe she can go get you something to wear."

"Samantha? She's not my friend. I don't even know her. What I will do is I'll wear your coat. That way it'll just look like you're my boyfriend. Like you're sweet, letting me wear your stuff in the cold."

"But then what?"

"What do you mean then what? Then I go home. Then you go home."

"And what about the coat?"

"I'll mail it to you. Or we can meet somewhere."

Ben knew it wouldn't work—he couldn't trust a girl like her. "Forget the coat for a minute. I'll go down and find your dress."

"You just said some drunks took it."

"Well, they did. But it was all wet so they dropped it. It's down there still, I'm sure of it."

"And if it's not?"

"Then we'll wrap you in my coat and get a cab."

"All right. But can you hurry? I feel like I'm going to get caught."

"You shouldn't feel that way. Nothing's happened."

"But it feels like it has. I feel dirty."

Ben shook his head. "Don't. I don't."

He was about to shut the door when she said, "Ben?"

"What is it?"

She tightened the towel around her body. "I'll still get paid, won't I?"

Ben smiled at her. "Of course," he said, and then shut the door and left.

He was just outside the hotel when he saw the old woman from the water fountain sitting on a bench where the taxis came. An old man sat beside her, his hand on her knee. The woman now had a paisley scarf around her neck and the man sported an old-timey pageboy hat. Both of them wore houndstooth coats. As Ben walked by, the woman jostled the man's arm. "Irving, it's that boy I was telling you about. The one who helped me with my bag."

The old man nodded and waved at Ben, who waved back but increased his pace, not wanting to get stuck in a conversation.

"Watch out for falling angels!" the old woman called to him. Before Ben was out of earshot, he heard the old man say, "I'm telling you, it wasn't an angel it was a *cat*. A white cat."

As he walked, Ben wondered what exactly the couple was doing sitting out in the cold. Perhaps they were waiting for a cab to take them to a late-night movie, during which one or the both of them would fall asleep. Later, in bed for the night, they would laugh about it. All that money spent just to take a nap in an uncomfortable chair. They would wear flannel pajamas and go to sleep with a perfunctory kiss on the lips. And they would be happy about it, for they would have not only the mild pleasure of the moment but also the severe pleasure of looking back on all they had shared together, a bounty of love that followed them everywhere they went, like the train of a wedding gown. Or perhaps they had not been waiting for a cab at all. Perhaps they had just been watching, enjoying the spectacle of people who populated the streets this time of night.

Ben kept walking. Eventually, he rounded the corner in the direction of the drunks who'd taken the girl's dress. He kept going until he came to a diner. It was one of those fluorescent establishments that glowed like a bug lamp after midnight. Ben thought of the framed *Nighthawks* print above Alana's kitchen table. She said it made her feel cozy, despite having learned in an art history class that it was meant to convey loneliness, isolation. Ben stopped and watched through the diner's front window as a man in a suit brought a forkful of pie to his mouth.

It was not until the man turned his head to cough that Ben saw it was Freddy. What was he doing at a diner? Ben looked to see if Freddy had at least gotten a beer, but where a pint should have been there was only a frosted glass of milk, inside of which stood a neon pink straw. He wondered where Samantha was—had Freddy left her in the room? But then the door to the bathroom opened and out she came.

Ben went into the diner, which smelled of fried potatoes and cleaning solution. He came up behind Freddy, who looked up from his pie, startled. "Ben," Freddy said, his face reddening. "What are you doing here?"

"What are *you* doing here?"

Freddy looked to Samantha, who was working on her own piece of pie. "Samantha was hungry. She didn't eat dinner."

Ben stared at their pie. Key lime. It seemed an odd choice. He'd always thought of key lime as a summer pie.

"Where's Kristin?" Freddy asked.

So, his girl had a name. Ben fidgeted in his coat. It was warm in the diner, but he could not simply set the coat on a stool—it would get dirty. "She had a headache," he said. "I was heading to the QuikTrip to get her some Advil."

"How sweet of you," Samantha said, smiling. "Hey, you want some pie?"

Ben looked at the pie and realized that somehow, despite the big meal, he was hungry. "That's okay," he said. "But thanks anyway."

After a moment of silence, Ben wished them both a good night. "Enjoy your pie," he said. On the way to the door he heard Freddy say, "You too," at which Samantha began to laugh. And that was that.

Ben wasn't sure what to make of this encounter. How long had Freddy and Samantha been at the diner? And why hadn't he thought of it—pie instead of whatever was supposed to happen in the hotel? Outside of the diner, he watched as Freddy set his fork down and drank the rest of his milk through the pink straw. Samantha had taken off her stilettos; her long toes gripped the stool's metal footrest.

Ben looked toward the hotel but began to walk the other way. He made it two blocks before he saw the dress. Someone had placed it over a parking meter, so that it took on a vaguely human shape. He touched it—the fabric was cold and wet. Suddenly, he couldn't stand the sight of it. He peeled it from the meter and chucked it as hard as he could into the limbs of a nearby Bradford pear tree. Alana hated Bradford pears—she thought they smelled like lady parts. Alana. He was, for the moment, relieved to think of her. Better her than the girl in the room—what was her name again?—whose dress now hung like a flag from the boughs of the tree. He liked seeing it there, far away from him, surrendering to the city he would soon abandon for a better life. And it would, he was certain, be a better life. A life that would fit him, that would not be muddled with people who did not fit him.

He buttoned his coat and continued on, toward home.

Stupid Girls

Point to any Saturday of my youth and there I'll be, with Ruby, drawn to her company out of equal parts love and boredom. This day was no exception. We were in Ruby's bedroom, which had, long ago, been her mother's. By now, it was Ruby's enough—jars of colorful sand, geode collection, a stack of *National Geographic* magazines—but there were certain fossils she refused to excavate: the Hershey's Kisses tin in which her mother had kept her earrings, the faded Beatles poster on the closet door. I'd never tell her, but I loved this room. You could feel the love seeping up from the carpet, condensing on the walls.

The plan was for Ruby to teach me how to give an old fashioned. This was a term only she used—everyone else at school called it a hand job—but Ruby was always behind in these ways. She'd pick up words from her Nana Faye without knowing they were from some long ago time, before MTV and IUDs, when girls wore pantyhose and didn't go to college. She'd say something like, *That dress is aces*, and I'd have to turn and act like I didn't know her. I figured I'd eventually have to cut her off, like a gangrenous limb, but for now she had a cucumber from Nana Faye's garden and was wagging it under my nose.

"You want to keep your hand moving," she said, showing me on the vegetable. "And spit on it when it gets dry."

"Where do you even go to do it?"

"What do you mean? They keep it in their pants."

"No, I mean, are you on a bed? The floor? How's the positioning is what I'm asking."

"Oh, I don't think they care, as long as you're touching it right."

"How'd you learn all this anyways?" I figured she'd read an article in *Seventeen*.

Ruby reddened. "Didn't I tell you? I met a man."

As far as I knew, the only men in Ruby's life were her podiatrist and her dermatologist, both prominent figures, as she was born with crooked bones in her toes and had a bald spot from where she pulled out her hair. The hair pulling was a nervous disease that worsened when she was stressed, and Ruby was always stressed. In class, she kept her fingers running across her head, so that by the time the bell rang there'd be a little hair critter under her desk—a tumbleweed of split ends and dandruff. *Don't forget your wire baby*, I'd tell her. The freshman boys had taken to calling her Patches.

"What do you mean you met a man?"

"Oh, you know how these things go." She waved a hand, as if we'd discussed this a thousand times.

"Ruby," I said. "What man?"

Her cheeks were pink—it was clear she'd been dying to tell me. "Just don't say anything mean about it, okay? If you do, I'll just think you're jealous."

"Will you just tell me already? We both know you're going to."

"Fine." She looked around, as if we were in a crowd and she needed to be coy. "He came around a couple weeks ago, delivering pizza. Nana Faye was at mah-jongg."

"The pizza guy?"

"See, I knew you'd think it's stupid. You're so predictable."

"I am not."

She laughed, started scraping a growth off the cucumber with her thumbnail.

"Ruby, you're telling me you lost your virginity to the pizza guy?"

"He's in *college*, Lottie. The pizza thing just pays the rent." This, as if paying the rent was something we, too, had to worry about. She took a piece of her hair and twisted it up around her thumb. Out came a few strands, which she sprinkled onto the ground. "See what you're making me do?"

"Chinese finger trap," I told her. This was supposed to make her clasp her hands together. "Well, what's he like then?"

She put her hands in her lap and began to slide the cucumber across her palm. "His name is Brandon. He goes to that little college next to the Expo center—the Catholic one. He already says he loves me."

"Don't you think it's a little weird? A guy that age?"

"Can't I like anyone who's not you?"

I wanted to protest but suddenly there was a noise at the door. Nana Faye. Before anything else, I saw the shoes—clunky leather loafers over pantyhose.

"What are you girls doing?" she asked. "What's the cucumber for?" For some reason, Nana Faye had done herself up, with mascara and purple eye shadow and tomato red lipstick. She looked like a hooker gone through a washing machine, but I wouldn't dare say it. I loved her.

"We were planning to make a salad," Ruby said, shaking the cucumber.

"In your bedroom?"

"We're *moving* to the kitchen."

"I told you not to fuddle around in that garden without asking. You'll bring bugs and they'll eat everything to shreds." With this she closed the door, so the ceramic mezuzah rattled. Ruby had tried to get rid of her mezuzah the year before, when we both decided we were agnostic—a scandal, in such a household—but Nana Faye found it in the trashcan and made Ruby kiss it eighteen times before nailing it back up.

"Don't you want to know what it was like?" Ruby asked. "The sex?"

"Not really," I said, not because I wasn't desperate to know, but because I was, perhaps for the first time ever, jealous of Ruby. Who would have thought someone like Ruby, with her little round teeth and her bald spots, would lose her virginity before me? You could have polled an audience of a thousand, a million, and all of them would have voted that I'd be the first. I wasn't a beauty queen, but I'd been told I had a nice figure and on occasion, if I was walking somewhere by myself, a passing car would honk and I'd turn to find a man—not attractive by any standard, but a man nonetheless—making kissy faces. While I'd kissed a total of four boys, two with tongue, I'd never come close to addressing the secret in their pants. To think of Ruby in the midst of such an adult act—to think her body even capable of it—was a shock to the system. But I could never tell her this, could never give her such a victory.

"Just so you know, it was bloody and it hurt like hell," Ruby said. "I could barely sit on a chair the next day. But it was also the best thing to ever happen to me. You really should try it sometime."

"You used protection, right?"

"Why would I? I'm on the pill."

"Since when?"

"Since forever. You know, there's stuff I don't tell you. Lots of stuff. Hadn't you ever thought of that?"

"Well, there's stuff you don't know about me, too. Don't think there's not."

"Like what?"

I scanned my mind. "I once let my cousin Harry look at my boobs. And then he grabbed them."

She busted out laughing; it was the wrong thing to say.

"I hope you get syphilis," I said. "And just so you know, it's obvious this guy is only using you." I then gathered my things and left, not even bothering to say good-bye to Nana Faye, who was clanking around the kitchen, making our dinner.

I spent the rest of the weekend waiting for Ruby to call, but that call never came. That we were fighting was not unusual. We fought often, about stupid things like her not returning my favorite sweater or why I didn't say something when the other girls laughed at her for running funny in gym class. But this fight was different. I could feel it.

I wasn't entirely worried, as our friendship had always felt like something that could live or die by my hands, not Ruby's. We were friends mostly because of inertia, because it would have taken more energy on my part to reverse our path and become enemies than to simply keep on with the friendship and its weekly sleepovers and study sessions and trips to the mall. There were more complicated moments, like the time at the seventh-grade Valentine's dance when Wesley Pittman asked me out as a joke, and Ruby—seeing the whole thing from the sidelines—came and swept me into a waltz. Or the time she told our Brownies leader, Miss Wheeler, that she, too, was allergic to horsehair and would have to stay behind while the rest of the troop rode off into the Flint Hills—then, too, the time she didn't laugh when I told her I was afraid of horses. I tried not to think about these times. It's a difficult trick for the young heart to love and hate at once—like trying to write the number six while you make clockwork circles with your foot.

Our friendship was, after all, a kind of arranged marriage, formed by my mother and Nana Faye when Ruby and I were ten years old. As the story went, they met at a temple luncheon. My mother and I were new to town, having just fled my father and his girlfriends in Topeka, and Ruby's parents had recently died in a car accident on the way to Oklahoma, where they were going to pick up a puppy for Ruby's birthday. Ruby was exhibiting strange behaviors: eating Q-tips, sleeping in cupboards, pushing pins into her teddy bear's privates. Nana Faye thought having a friend might help her. And so, like a piece of ugly new furniture, she appeared in my mother's house with an invisible nametag that read DELIVERY FOR LOTTIE. Even then, my instinct was to dislike her. She smelled funny, like an old pillowcase, and always had snot coming out of her nose. At school she ate lunch alone, by the trashcans, or in the counselor's office.

I had always thought of our friendship as having an expiration date, but the truth was I needed Ruby. She was an escape, a door out of my own life and into one more comfortable. I didn't much like my own house or my own mother, who was too busy finding a replacement for my father to pay any real attention to me. It was clear we were better off on our own, but still she kept on, like a kid trying to put a milk tooth back in the socket.

Ruby's house, on the other hand, was always clean and quiet. Nana Faye liked to burn candles and would, at the beginning of every season, give me bags of clothes Ruby didn't want anymore. If Ruby and I were sad or bored or just had ants in our pants, she'd take us out for hot fudge sundaes or to get our makeup done at Dillard's. If we were really good, she'd flatten our hair—a long, luxurious process that involved spreading our curls onto a beach towel so that she could glide a hot iron across them, the warmth rushing up to our necks. Marcia Brady hair, she called it. Sometimes I thought of Nana Faye as a lighthouse, my mother as a boat with a hole in the bottom. And what was Ruby? Sometimes the lightbulb. Sometimes the darkness.

I didn't see Ruby until Monday when, as usual, I took the desk beside her in biology.

"We were supposed to see a movie on Sunday," I told her. She was wearing her hair in a way she never had before—two small braids that met in the back to form a single strand that concealed her bald spot.

"I was busy," she said. "Treating my syphilis."

I didn't know what to say, so I said nothing.

"Anyways, I already went to the movies with Brandon. We saw the new Bond movie." She narrowed her eyes, to show she knew exactly how much she was hurting me.

"Was it any good?" I asked, trying to sound unfazed.

She flipped her hair behind her shoulder. I noticed that a boy on the other end of the classroom was looking at her. "Who knows?" she said. "We barely watched it."

Normally, I'd go to Ruby's after school. We'd do our homework and Nana Faye would feed us popcorn or pizza bagels until *Jeopardy!* came on at six. But Ruby wasn't out by the Dumpsters, where we usually met, so I walked home by myself.

The weatherman had predicted severe storms, with a chance of tornadoes in the late afternoon. The sky did look a bit green, the pea soup color that made my stomach feel hollow. I wondered what Ruby was doing. She was deathly afraid of tornadoes. Whenever the sirens went off, she'd gather her most precious possessions—a composition notebook in which her father had written poems and lists (groceries, errands, songs he'd heard on the radio), and a nearly empty bottle of her mother's Chanel No. 5—and head to the bathroom in the basement, where she'd sit in the bathtub with Nana Faye's favorite Navajo blanket pulled over her head and an old crank radio tuned to the weather report. I could picture her half-running the mile back to her house, tears welling in her eyes as the wind stirred up little cyclones of leaves. Served her right. We'd been talking about seeing the new Bond movie for months.

At home, I hesitated in front of the door. I didn't want to go in, but I had nowhere else to go.

Inside, my mother was rustling through the hall closet. "Lottie, have you seen my umbrella?" she asked. "The good one?" Her hair was different—the stripe of gray filled in, frizzy ends rolled into glossy cigars.

"It's not raining yet," I told her.

"But it might rain later. And Gary's taking me to Scotch and Sirloin after the movie. I don't want to ruin my hair if it rains."

"They won't kick you out for having wet hair."

"But I want to look nice. I think this might be the night—he's been talking about needing to settle down. Oh God, I'm nervous. Do I look nervous? Is my hair all right?"

"Christ," I said. For the past two months, every one of their dates had started out as an occasion for a proposal, and every one had ended with a fight.

They were a terrible match. Gary liked fly-fishing and quail hunting and had voted Republican in every election since Johnson; my mother liked the Home Shopping Network and was known for going around the neighborhood collecting VOTE BUSH signs, scraping his name from bumper stickers with a spoon. But none of this mattered because she was a lonely substitute teacher and we were poor and Gary had money and a big old empty life that needed a woman to clean it. And so she ignored his snoring and his worsening diabetes—he'd already gone blind in one eye—and the fact that one night I woke to find him at the door of my bedroom, a hand in his waistband. In the morning, he made a big production about how he'd woken up in the middle of the front yard with a hunk of deli meat in his hand—sleepwalking.

"Why are you even here?" my mother asked, still searching around the closet. "I thought you'd be at Ruby's. There's nothing for you to eat here."

"It's fine—I'll just starve to death."

"Eureka," she said, and came out with an umbrella just as the doorbell buzzed.

Gary's arrival was never a minor affair. He came to us like a prince visiting a hovel, making sure my mother and I hadn't fallen victim to the various dangers of living alone as women. Once inside, he would perform a scan of the house, looking for things to fix—anything to prove we were living in shambles. "God almighty, Jody, this light fixture's ancient," he'd say, and then snap it from the wall so that a cloud of dust and dead moths would float to the floor like gothic confetti. He'd promise to bring a new one the next time he came over, but he never did, and so it would be up to my mother to replace whatever it was with money she did not have. Currently, he was fiddling with the doorbell.

"Makes a strange noise, doesn't it? Not so much a ding-dong as an eeek-akkk." He hailed from Kentucky and had an accent that reminded me of cornbread and grits. *Doesn't it* came out *duddnit*. Ruby called him Colonel Sanders.

"Oh, it's fine," my mother said, trying to pull him from the door. "It makes a noise. That's what it's supposed to do."

"I'll bring my tool kit next time. Do some rewiring." He then looked at me and back to my mother. "I thought you said she'd be at Ruby's."

"That's what I thought, too."

I hated when they talked like this, as if I were on the other side of a glass panel. "Ruby had plans," I said.

"Plans that don't involve you?" my mother said. "That's new."

"Sounds like someone's got a boyfriend," Gary said, and winked at me. He loved to have a reason to wink at me.

The idea of Ruby having a boyfriend made my mother laugh. "I'm sorry," she said. "I'm being mean. I'm sure Ruby's the talk of the town. Anyways, we should get going."

Once they were gone, I pulled a tub of Moose Tracks from the freezer and ate it with a grapefruit spoon. It was meant to cheer me up, but instead I felt bloated and ugly. I'd been told by more than one authority figure (my mother and Miss Hawthorne, the gym teacher) that I should watch what I eat. *Curves are hot but fat is not.* Their concern was not unjustified. I had a rash on the inside of my thighs from where my legs rubbed, and you could grab a generous handful of meat from my hips. But my desire for food was as strong as my desire for beauty. Little made me happier than a warm biscuit or an appointment in front of the television with a bowl of cheddar and sour cream Ruffles. What else in life was as loyal, as predictably satisfying as food? Certainly not people. Definitely not Ruby.

I let half an hour pass before I called her. She answered on the first ring, as if she'd been waiting by the telephone. I took this as a good sign and asked if she wanted to do something—watch a movie, walk to the Walgreens to try on nail polish.

"I thought I told you I was busy," she said.

"Well, you answered the phone, didn't you?"

"That doesn't mean I'm not busy."

I didn't want to ask but I had to. "Are you hanging out with Brandon tonight?"

"Lottie," she said. "Is it so hard to imagine I'd rather be alone than hang out with you?"

Before I could say anything, she hung up.

My mother kept the Yellow Pages on the bookshelf, between the *Webster's* dictionary and a photo album of her and my dad's honeymoon. When I pulled it out, a fine layer of dust came with it. I set it down on the table and turned randomly to the V section. The first thing I saw was WHIRLTECH VACUUMS.

The man who answered sounded young enough. His voice was low, like a rumble of thunder. I made my voice deeper, more mature, and explained that I was looking for a new vacuum. A friend of mine told me how much she loved her new WhirlTech. "I was wondering if you could come by and do a demo," I said.

On the other end, I could hear the background noise of the store—a jingle bell ringing above a door and the drone of small talk. "What's your address ma'am?" the salesman asked.

I hurried to put on blush and perfume. In the bathroom, I consulted my reflection and tried to assess exactly how pretty I was. It was a difficult task, like asking: Are trees pretty? Are thunderclouds ugly? At some point, a thing simply looked how it looked. But here I was, on the cusp of something big. And I did look pretty. I had to, or I'd never have the courage to do what needed to be done. I smiled to myself in the mirror. A dental hygienist once told me that my smile was *dazzling*.

When the doorbell rang, I smoothed my hair and took a deep breath before opening the door. On the other side stood a man with a vacuum. He was tall—too tall for my taste—with broad shoulders and a decent chin. He was maybe late twenties, early thirties—not the worst, but not the best either. On his shirt was a nametag that read EARL, an unfortunate detail that could be easily forgotten, along with his eyes, which were wide set and sort of dopey looking, like a sloth's. If you focused on his Adam's apple, he was halfway to handsome.

"Is your mother home?" asked Earl.

"You know, she *just* ran out for a quick errand, but she'll be back soon." I smiled and pushed out my chest. "Come in and wait if you want."

He grabbed his gear and followed me inside, where he appeared many times larger than he had on the porch. He stooped over, as if the ceiling threatened to come down on him. His let his arms dangle and fidget, as if afraid they might, at any moment, lash out and break something.

"Want to sit?" I asked.

He looked at the couch and lowered himself carefully, as if trying not to cause an atmospheric disturbance. "Are you sure your mom'll be back soon? I don't mind coming back another day."

"Any minute, now. Really."

I wasn't sure how to stall, how to talk to someone like him. Aside from the eye doctor, I had never had this before—the private company of an adult man I didn't know. I played up my maturity, crossing my legs and asking him if he'd like some coffee, although I'd never made coffee in my life.

"I could go for a cup," he said. "Black is fine."

I told him all right, but made no move toward the kitchen and hoped that he would forget about it.

"So, something happen to your mother's vacuum?" he asked.

"It's the funniest thing. It just broke down all of sudden. Made a weird smell and started eating up the carpet."

"Well, that's just the thing this machine won't do—you probably don't know much about vacuums yet, huh? You're just a girl. But it's an investment, really. The average woman spends more than a grand on vacuums throughout her life. They buy cheap, and then they have to keep replacing it every year or two. But this thing," he petted the vacuum like it was a dear old golden retriever, "it'll last a lifetime. That's what the guarantee's for."

"Sounds fantastic," I said, thinking only that he called me a girl— *just a girl.*

"Oh, it is fantastic. You'll see when I do the demo. Do you mind if I get things ready for when your mom comes home?"

"Go for it," I told him, and then watched as he opened a duffel bag from which he extracted three glass mason jars. He placed the jars carefully on the coffee table and pointed to each. "Dirt, sand, glitter," he said. "Last one usually seals the deal. Especially in households with children. Do you have any younger siblings?"

I shook my head, feigning interest as he made three separate piles—dirt, sand, and glitter—and rubbed each into the carpet with a gentle circular motion. I thought of Ruby in bed with Brandon, his body poised over her, his hands on the soft flesh of her tummy.

Earl sat down and began to assemble the vacuum, fitting tubes onto a long, rubber hose that extended from the machine's round body. I scooted closer to him, so that I could smell his laundry detergent.

Beneath this, he smelled of sweat, of hours spent lugging equipment from door to door. He didn't seem to notice that we were touching, that my thigh was pressed against his. My heart raced as he attached a thin plastic wand to the end of the hose and screwed it tight.

"All set," he said.

"You sure you don't need anything else?" Again, I pressed my thigh into his, hard enough that he would have to notice. For a moment I thought he might play dumb, but then suddenly, as if I'd activated a switch, he sprang into action—his lips on my lips, his hands everywhere at once, probing and grabbing. Then his mouth was on my neck—my neck! It tickled, and I couldn't help but giggle. How funny, I thought, to go from point A to B so quickly, and without words. Like alchemy: a stranger into a lover, a friend into an enemy.

"It was you on the phone. Wasn't it?" he asked, his voice like gravel in my ear. His grip around my waist tightened and he began to move his hand down, inward, toward the hem of my jean shorts. "Wasn't it?" he repeated, more forcefully.

"It was," I said, trying to sound sexy, but it came out small and high-pitched.

"I could tell you wanted it all along. I could tell you were bad. Real bad."

"You could?"

"Honey, you've got sex written in bold across your forehead. The worst ones always do."

I reveled in the idea of this sex marquee. If my forehead said sex, what did Ruby's say? Mayonnaise? One-room schoolhouse?

Up close, I could see a faint yellow stain around his shirt collar. I wondered if his mother taught him to do wash, like Nana Faye had taught me, or if he had a girlfriend at home to do it for him. Suddenly there were a million details I didn't see before, important details that Ruby probably knew about Brandon: Where was he born? Where were his grandparents born? Did he have any siblings? Any pets? Had he ever been camping? Skiing? Horseback riding? Why was he selling vacuums? Did he ever dream of leaving Wichita? Leaving Kansas?

"Have you ever been to Colorado?" I asked him.

He stopped moving. "What's that?"

"Colorado. You ever been? I've got an aunt who lives there but I've never visited. My mom says if we went I'd probably spend the whole trip puking because of the altitude."

He frowned and leaned in, started kissing me again. "Fuck Colorado," he said, and that's when I felt his hardness against me. Terrifying. I suddenly dreaded the moment when he would take off his pants. He was sweating now, beads of moisture trailing from his hairline to his cheek. Panting. Moaning. I thought of Ruby, how she'd handled all of this: Where did she put her hands? What did she say? How did she move?

He pinched the bottom of my shirt and lifted it over my head, exposing my pink cotton bra. The bra was a reject of Ruby's and was reinforced with a generous layer of padding. In a matter of seconds, both it and my underwear were on the floor, and Earl's mouth—a mouth that ate what, I did not know, that brushed how many times a day, I did not know, that spoke how many languages, I did now know—was exploring my breasts, tasting a part of my body that nobody had ever tasted, and which only my mother and a few select doctors had ever seen. And Ruby. Aside from my mother, Ruby was the only person I openly changed in front of, the only person who had seen me naked. I thought then of the time Nana Faye took us shopping for dresses for the Valentine's dance—the same dance where Wesley Pittman asked me out as a joke. Ruby nearly burst a lung trying to get into a horrendous red dress that had shoulder pads—shoulder pads!—and a garish bow that tied in the back. When it was all done she looked like a Christmas present gone wrong, but Nana Faye choked up when she saw her. "You look just like your mother," she'd said, tears welling in her eyes. At the dance, Minnie McDonough from the pep squad asked me where Ruby had found such an ugly dress. "Probably dug it out of her mother's grave," I told her. Minnie had smiled and said, "How deliciously mean." I'd never forgotten that word, *deliciously*, as if my meanness were a piece of candy for Minnie to pop in her mouth. Now, Ruby was the one in love—*He already says he loves me*—and I was the one in the ugly red dress.

Earl had just moved in for the kill—an explosion of pain so fierce I couldn't really believe it—when I heard myself whisper, "I love you."

"What?" Earl asked, a hint of alarm in his voice. "What'd you just say?"

My body burned with heat. There was pain, large and immediate as an oncoming train, and only beyond this—like a tiny bird skating the horizon—the faintest outline of pleasure. I didn't want him to stop, but he already had. "Nothing," I told him. "It was a sneeze."

He burrowed his head into my chest and let out an exasperated sound. "Oh, Christ," he said, and then got up and grabbed for his clothes, muttering something about being stupid. Stupid vacuums. Stupid girls. Soon his pants were on, his belt buckled. Only then did it occur to me that he hadn't used protection.

"This never happened," he said, gesturing to me, to my naked body. "You don't tell anyone, I don't tell anyone. Got it?"

I didn't know what to say. My tongue was a dead thing, dry and dusty in my mouth.

Eventually the front door opened and closed. He was already out of earshot when I asked, "Where are you going?" He'd left the vacuum behind and it stared at me with its singular, prehistoric eye. A monster from another world.

Everything grew still—as static as a bulb growing deep underground. This is how I felt: like an onion bulb, naked and smooth and surrounded by dirt. Alone. For a moment, I felt as if I might burst open, shoot green tendrils from my fingertips until they found Ruby—her fingers, her wrist, her neck. I wanted to call her and tell her what had happened, but of course I couldn't. There was nobody I could talk to, not a single person in the entire world. Eventually, I felt an itch beneath my right big toe. Outside, a mourning dove began to coo.

There was little to think of that did not hurt, and so I focused instead on the carpet. In his exit, Earl had stomped in the pile of glitter, sending up a cloud of sparkling debris. How pretty, I thought, letting my mind focus on the glitter. I knew that at some point, I would have to get up and clean it.

Thousand-Dollar Decoy

In the dream, the mallard on Elliot's chest weighs a hundred pounds, if not a thousand. It is crushing his lungs. He cannot breathe. He tries to turn, but he cannot turn. He cannot even move—the mallard is too heavy. It smells of algae and cut grass and is not without a hint of cuteness, the curve of its yellow beak forming a timid smile. Its eyes are liquid black and in them Elliot's terror is reflected back to him. In time, he discovers that his hands are free. With great effort, he brings them to the mallard's green neck. The iridescent feathers are smooth as skin beneath his grip. Elliot squeezes as hard as he can. He knows his life depends on it.

When he wakes, he finds that he is strangling his girlfriend, Alice. A low gurgling noise bubbles up from her throat and fills their dark studio apartment. This is only their first night in the apartment. Most of their possessions are still in the cardboard boxes that line the wall opposite their bed. Before they went to sleep, Alice had listed off all the things she wanted to do in the morning: hang pictures, assemble the closet organizer, locate her mother's china to make sure nothing had broken. Then, they had made love. Elliot had felt light with happiness as he drifted into sleep, Alice in his arms. Everything was exactly as he wanted it to be, down to the placement of the bed, which was centered against a wall instead of pressed into a corner to economize space. He'd never lived with a woman before, but now he was with Alice—*living* with Alice—and the bed belonged to both of them, an equal possession that required equal access. They were adults, and they were in love. They were sharing a bed. They each had their own nightstand.

They'd chosen the apartment because it was located exactly between their two jobs. Alice was a nurse in an oncology ward and Elliot inspected children's toys. When he told people what he did, they imagined him wearing overalls and a hardhat, examining racecars and baby dolls as they passed by on a conveyor belt. In truth, he had a PhD and worked in a lab. The winter before, he'd detected a potentially lethal amount of lead in a popular play food set. Alice liked to see him dressed for work, in his white lab coat and plastic goggles.

They'd met at a wedding, a fact Alice hated. If she had it her way, they would have met somewhere more interesting, perhaps at a symposium on fireflies or a hostel in Cambodia—anything for a better story. The wedding was painfully average. Alice's friend Heather was marrying a cousin of Elliot's, and both bride and groom were known for being boring, to the point where it was a sort of joke among their friends. A few people had even gone in on a gift card to Applebee's. The wedding was nearly unbearable—the Catholic ceremony was an hour too long and filled with the steady weeping of a large woman who held a silk handkerchief to her face, as if it might contain the sound. When the guests finally gathered for the apology of dinner, a sigh of disappointment circled the room when it was discovered that it would be a dry reception. What a treat, then, to find Alice. She was seated beside Elliot, who could not help but smile as her knee occasionally knocked against his. She told joke after joke, glowing like a lantern in the otherwise dreary reception hall. One man—a ruddy, balding creature with thick glasses that magnified his eyes—laughed so hard at one of her stories that he coughed a mass of green food back onto his plate, as if he were a giant baby. After dinner, Elliot mustered the courage to ask Alice to dance.

That was more than two years ago. Now he struggles in the comfort of their bed—really her bed, brought over from her apartment upon the agreement that hers was more comfortable than his—his hands clasped around her perfect throat. When he lets go, she whimpers. He knows it is the sound of everything he loves coming to a close.

After a moment of paralysis, she scrambles from the bed and runs to the bathroom and shuts the door. In the dark, Elliot sees only the strip of light coming from the bottom of the door and the shadow of her feet moving on the other side. He pulls himself from bed and goes to the door. He knocks.

"Go away," she says.

"Alice. I was dreaming."

"I said go away."

"Please, Alice. There was a mallard—it was suffocating me." He realizes how ridiculous this sounds. Why mallard? Why not duck? "I would never hurt you."

There is only silence, and then the sound of running water. Unsure what to do, Elliot goes back to bed, where he pinches the skin on his arms over and over again. Without meaning to, he falls asleep.

In the morning, there is still the strip of light under the bathroom door. Alice has slept in the tub, using a balled up bath towel as a pillow. She tells him this as she sits across from him at the breakfast table. He has made her French toast, her favorite, but she refuses to eat. She is not hungry. There are purple bags beneath her eyes and she smells sour, like curdled milk. Still, Elliot wants to kiss her, to suck the bruise from her neck and into his own body, to have it settle into the muscle of his heart. He would endure this bruise forever if it meant the one on her neck would disappear.

"I can't be here today," she tells him.

He tries to stay calm. "Okay. But what about the apartment? They're delivering the couch today." This is a lie—the couch is not set to arrive for another couple of days, but for a moment he believes that the couch can save them. It is their most expensive purchase—a horrendous red sectional from Pottery Barn. It took them weeks to finally choose one. He'd wanted something dark and leather, but Alice said she would rather go back to living alone than have to look at leather every day. To prove her point, she started looking up studios on Craigslist. She went so far as to tour two apartments, one of which she rather liked, before Elliot finally gave in.

"I'm going out," she says. "I'll come home when I'm ready."

He has no choice but to watch as she gathers her things. He is not the type to beg or make a fuss, a characteristic Alice has always faulted him for. She herself is quick to argue with others—family, friends, baristas, and bank tellers—and expects Elliot to back her up, even if he doesn't agree with her point. Of course, it's never about defending her point, but about defending *her*. "You'd sit back in the trenches and watch me get shot up," Alice once told him, after a particularly bad argument she'd had with one of their mutual friends in which Elliot stood by, eating a plateful of miniature hotdogs. Elliot argued that he wouldn't even be on the battlefield to begin with. He'd be off somewhere else—in a neutral country, like Sweden, eating cream puffs or watching a peace parade. She then compared him to the Germans who ignored the smell of smoke from the crematoriums. "You'd let millions of people die to avoid being bothered," she'd said, emphasizing this last word—*bothered*.

Now, he follows her into their bedroom, where she packs a duffel bag with T-shirts and pajama pants and underwear. She then goes to the bathroom. He knows he is in trouble if she takes her shaving cream; she only shaves once a week, on Sunday nights. When she is finally packed and gone—out of the apartment without even a kiss good-bye—he inspects the bathroom. The shaving cream is gone, as is the shampoo and conditioner and the little contraption she uses to curl her eyelashes. Even the bath towel is missing.

Elliot has called Alice sixteen times since she left the day before. It is the weekend, and so he has nothing to do but wait for the phone to ring, for the door to open, for time to rewind so he can undream his dream. Why couldn't the mallard have been a butterfly? Or a kitten? Why, for that matter, had there been a mallard at all? The only mallard he can even think of is the wooden one his stepfather, Roy, keeps on the highest shelf of his home office. It was an expensive mallard, hand painted by a popular folk artist in Jackson Hole, where Roy and his first wife, Barbie, lived before she was diagnosed with leukemia.

The artist had given them a discount, but even then it was pricey. A thousand dollars. Elliot's mother has always loved the mallard, which she often refers to as "the avian sculpture." She once asked Roy to put it on the dining room table so that they could enjoy it during meals. Roy refused, saying a thousand-dollar decoy had no place on a dining room table. Once, Elliot caught him whispering to the decoy, "Barbie Doll, I miss you."

Now that he has remembered Roy's wooden mallard, Elliot cannot stop thinking about it. He wants to see the mallard, to hold it in his hands and feel whether it is heavy or light, smooth or textured. What kind of person buys a thousand-dollar decoy?

Elliot wishes he had the distraction of work to look forward to, but it is the weekend before Thanksgiving and he's taken the whole week off. Alice and he made plans to spend the holiday with his parents in Wichita. He wonders if this little stint will last until Thursday morning, when they are due to drive out. He cannot believe that it will, and so he waits. He tells himself he is virtuous for being patient.

To pass the time, he arranges the apartment without her. He goes through his own boxes first, organizing his books on the bookshelf and putting his dishes into their proper cabinets. He constructs two matching IKEA end tables and puts them on either side of where the couch will eventually go, once it is delivered. He can imagine the couch taking the place of the emptiness, just as he can imagine Alice returning, replacing the quiet apartment with the sound of her voice, her laughter. She is the kind of woman who sings when she is happy— any song that comes to her mind. "Pop Goes the Weasel." "Sometimes When We Touch." The jingle for the Starlight Drive-In. Sometimes her singing drives Elliot crazy, but he does not remember this now. Nor does he remember the time he put a hand over her mouth and told her to be silent. Or how she bit his finger in response.

This is not the first time something like the mallard dream has happened, but Alice does not know this. It happened once before, when Elliot was only a boy. He'd been taking a nap with his cousin, Olivia, on their grandmother's living room floor. He remembers the green shag carpet and his grandmother's shih tzu, Dolly, sniffing the perimeter of where he and Olivia lay belly-up on an old down comforter.

His mother had turned out the lights and forced the adults from the living room so the children could rest. They had to sleep in the living room because Elliot was frightened of the bedrooms. His father had died in one of them when Elliot was only a baby—which room, he was never told, but he knew it had happened in this house, in one of the beds, while his father was sleeping. And so it was on the floor of his grandmother's living room that Elliot had woken to find that he was pummeling Olivia's face with the palms of his hands. The adults had come in screaming—they pulled him off his cousin and made him sit alone in the master bedroom, perhaps the most haunted of all the rooms. Alone, he was forced to recall the dream. There had been a man sitting on his chest, his head bloated to the size of a pumpkin. The man had a skinny white tongue that he kept running across his lips, as if he were thirsty. He was wearing the same plaid button-down Elliot's father wore in the picture his mother kept above the fireplace.

And now there was this, the mallard. How could he ever trust himself again? He wonders what else he might do in his sleep, what other crimes he might commit. Of course, Alice must be thinking the same thing. And so he is not entirely surprised when she does not come home that day, or the next. She does not answer his calls. Desperate, he calls her sister, who picks up and says, "Hello?" only to then hang up when a male voice in the background shouts, "She explicitly told us not to talk to him, Marta. Can't you do anything right?"

He has loved Alice thoroughly since he met her, and the idea of living without her is almost too difficult a thought to bear. Outside of this, her absence also poses several logistical problems. The most immediate of these is Thanksgiving with his parents. The second is how he will pay rent, which is affordable if split between the two of them but which will drain him if he has to carry the burden alone.

And so he goes to the only place he thinks she could be hiding.

Alice's ex-girlfriend's name is Ramona, and she is the kind of woman who makes Elliot want to join a gym. She is not a beautiful woman—her face is acne scarred and dominated by a large, crooked nose—but she danced for the Kansas City ballet before settling into a career as a physical therapist. When she answers the door, she does so wearing sweatpants rolled down to reveal the blades of her hipbones. There in the background, sitting on the couch in her favorite pair of flannel pajamas, is Alice. Her hair is done up in a messy ponytail and she is wearing her glasses, the ones he spent hours helping her pick out at the optometrist's office. She'd been a pain that day, making absurd claims about her appearance. *My face is too small. I just don't have the same eyebrows I used to.*

He knows Ramona's address because Alice commented on the building every time they drove by. She had made a point not to look at apartments near it, claiming she'd rather pay higher rent than see Ramona every time she went for a jog.

Elliot does not know exactly how or why Alice and Ramona's relationship ended. From what he's gathered, they were deeply in love until one day, while they were walking downtown, Alice saw Ramona kick an empty soda can toward a homeless man who was sitting on the corner. Perhaps it had been an accident—Alice never did ask Ramona about it—but Alice couldn't shake the feeling that Ramona had kicked the can on purpose. Was it possible she'd spent years of her life loving a woman who was capable of such a simple cruelty? Eventually, Alice asked for a break. She needed space, some time to think and unremember the sound of the can skipping across concrete. It was during this break that she met Elliot.

"Let me talk to her," he says to Ramona, who is trying to block Elliot's view into the apartment.

"She doesn't want to talk to you. If she did, she would have called you. Or answered one of your thousands of calls."

"Alice," Elliot calls from the doorway. "Alice, just give me five minutes. I think you at least owe me five minutes."

Ramona begins to close the door, but Alice finally appears behind her. "What do you want?" she asks.

Ramona gives up and retreats into the apartment. Now it is just him and Alice in the doorway. He wants to grab her, to kiss her and reclaim her as his own. But deep down, he knows that it is too late for this. He knows without knowing that his time with Alice is over.

"I want you to come to Thanksgiving," he says. "My parents are still expecting you."

She looks down to her bare feet. "I'm not coming anymore," she says. "I'm sorry."

"Will you at least come home so we can talk about it? I understand if you don't want to sleep with me for a while, but we can go slow, step by step. I want you to come home. You don't have to come to Thanksgiving, but I want you to come home. Please. All of our stuff— they've delivered the couch. It's a good couch. You should at least come back to see it. I only got it because of you, you know. I wanted the other one. The leather. But I did it for you. Because I love you."

Alice looks back into the apartment, where Ramona has taken her place on the couch, which is shabby and a horrendous shade of green. Her bare feet are up on the coffee table and she's drinking a cup of coffee, watching the two of them at her door. In the corner is an armchair. Tan leather.

"I'm sorry," Alice says.

"But your stuff."

"I don't even want to think about it. Not yet."

"But everything was fine," he manages to say. "Everything was so good—you didn't even give it a chance. The apartment is still ours. And the couch—"

She reaches up and rubs her neck, which is bruised a faint purple. "I just can't," she says. "I'm sorry. I really am, even if you don't believe me."

"But it was only a dream," he says.

"I know," she says. "But I was there. I was really there."

"What about the apartment?" he says. It is all he can find to say.

"I'm sorry," she says, and then gently shuts the door.

Back at the apartment, he unpacks the rest of her things. He hangs her blouses in the closet and puts her shoes on the shoe rack, allowing each item to fill his head with a different memory. Her perfumes go on a little mirrored tray she inherited from her grandmother the spring before. He cannot help but spray some of her favorite scent onto his wrist, which he brings to his nose for the remainder of the day. Soon, the apartment belongs to the both of them again. Her favorite coffee mug sits on the end table, arguing for her imminent return. Her notebooks are stacked on the kitchen table. Her mother's china is in the display cabinet.

Thursday arrives too soon. When he leaves the apartment, he does so reluctantly. He has grown fond of the space, of seeing his and Alice's things comingling on the shelves and in the cabinets and the drawers. He's sprayed the couch cushions with her perfume, and every afternoon he takes a long, dreamless nap.

When he arrives at his parents' house, they are alarmed to find that Alice is not with him; he has not told them about the dream, about Ramona. He is, in turn, alarmed to find that his parents have both grown younger since he last saw them. His mother has dyed her hair the color of a rose and found a new kind of makeup that makes her skin look dewy and soft. Roy has lost fifteen pounds by eliminating desserts—a fact that this mother brings up at random intervals, chanting, *Fifteen pounds! Fifteen pounds! Can you believe it?* as she pats Roy's stomach. Roy is back in the clothes he wore when Elliot was in high school, the plaid shirts tucked into tight blue jeans, a kind of urban cowboy look that Elliot tried and failed to mimic as an adult, opting instead for an endless combination of earth-tone T-shirts and khakis, wool sweaters, and boat shoes.

"So is Alice coming later in the weekend?" his mother eventually asks. She has never liked Alice, whom she once caught checking the price tag on a bottle of wine Roy bought for dinner. Elliot tried to convince her that Alice had merely liked the wine and was checking to see if it was something they could afford for themselves, but of course his mother didn't buy this. If there was one thing his mother believed in, it was her ability to read other people. As the story went, she'd known his father was sick before he'd even felt symptoms; she was the one who told him to go to the doctor, to get the scans. She had also known that Roy, one of Elliot's father's best friends, would wait exactly a year before confessing his love to her.

"No, she's not coming," Elliot says, and something in his tone must tell her not to ask any more questions, because Alice is not brought up again until after the Thanksgiving meal. He and his parents have eaten nearly an entire turkey between the three of them, along with most of a large porcelain bowl full of sweet potatoes that Elliot notices are not actually sweet this year but instead taste like earth with a hint of nutmeg. Still, he eats two servings, along with three buttered rolls, a mountain of green bean casserole, and a portion of glazed ham that would have satisfied an entire table of children. He is sleepy and morose and uncomfortably full when his mother directs him to the living room couch and sits down beside him. "Okay," she says. "Where's Alice?"

Caught off guard, Elliot cannot help but begin to cry. It is the first time he's shared his grief with anyone, and the fact that it is his mother makes him return to his boyhood, when something as small as a splinter would send him running into her arms. "I had a dream," he begins, and then explains the rest. As he talks, he wonders if his stepfather is somewhere nearby, listening. While his mother and Roy were setting the table, he'd snuck into Roy's study to confront the mallard. He hadn't intended to do anything—he just wanted to look at it—but the sight of the mallard enraged him. He'd grabbed the mallard and gone to the yard, where he'd hurled it over the fence. There was a satisfying plop as it landed in the McBrides' swimming pool. His mother had found him just moments after, standing by the fence. When she asked what he was doing he told her he was checking to see if a carving he'd done as a boy was still in the fence. "Well, is it?" she'd asked. He'd frozen, unsure of how to answer. "No," he'd said. "It's gone."

When he finishes explaining about Alice—about the dream and the mallard and Ramona—his mother begins to laugh. "I'm sorry," she says, still laughing. "I just can't help it. You blame Roy? And his avian sculpture?"

"Yes," he says, only now realizing that it's the truth. "I do."

"All right," his mother says, and pats his knee as if he is once again just a young boy with a boo-boo. "All right. I won't take that from you."

"You're making it sound like there's something I'm not accepting."

"You were dreaming," she says, her tone suddenly serious. "You were asleep, Elliot. Who could blame you for something you did while you were sleeping?"

"I left bruises on her neck. She's terrified of me."

"Love isn't a china doll," she says. "It's a monster. If it was that easy to get out of it, we'd all be alone."

"You're saying she never loved me."

"Not that she never loved you, but that maybe she hasn't for a while. That's all. I know it hurts." She pats his leg again.

"You don't care at all, do you?"

"Of course I do, I'm your mother." She pauses, gives his leg a final squeeze. "Do you want pie? There's pumpkin pie."

"You're so frustrating sometimes," he says. "I could get in my car and go home right now if I really wanted to." As soon as he says it, he wonders how he didn't think of it earlier. What had he been thinking, coming all this way, leaving the apartment unattended? What if Alice decided to return? What if, knowing he wouldn't be there, she came and collected her things?

"Don't be dramatic," his mother says. With this she gets up and goes to the kitchen, leaving Elliot alone on the couch. A moment later she calls from the kitchen, "Do you want a big slice or a little slice?"

"Big," Elliot says. "And whipped cream."

He then goes to his room—his childhood room, with the twin bed and the ugly alien spaceship Roy painted above his window long ago, without Elliot's permission—and gets his bag in order. Soon, he will be back in the apartment with Alice's things—her necklaces, her toaster oven, her collection of miniature animal figurines. Where he will put the mallard, he still hasn't decided. For now, he hurries to the bathroom to gather his toiletries. He flushes the toilet so that his mother will think he has simply gone to the bathroom, that this is why he is not still sitting on the couch, waiting patiently for her to return with his pie. Neither she nor Roy will think about the mallard until they run into Mr. McBride, perhaps while getting the mail or pumping gas at the QuikTrip. "Elliot came by to get some kind of duck thing," Mr. McBride will tell them. "Still don't understand how it got in my pool, but stranger things have happened."

First Love

Jett Kaplan decided it was time he had sexual relations. Everyone else was doing it. Bill Clinton had done it, which implied that Monica Lewinsky had also done it. Even Chance LaBouda, who was an entire year younger than Jett and who once admitted to tongue kissing his grandmother's miniature schnauzer, even he had just made it with that gap-toothed sophomore Vicky Romano. So why not Jett? Certainly it was his turn. He was as good-looking as any fourteen-year-old boy had a right to be. Sure, his hair turned greasy in a matter of hours and the stubble above his lip had conspired into an upsetting suggestion of puberty, but he was on his way to handsomeness—he was sure of it. All he had to do was look at his father to see that good looks awaited him somewhere down the road. He imagined it this way, his taking a stroll and suddenly coming upon a parcel with the words HANDSOMENESS FOR JETT! written on the side. He would open it to the delight of his father, who had a full head of feathery hair and green eyes that made women at Kmart turn to look. That would be him one day, Jett was sure of it. Until then, wasn't he entitled to some practice runs? Certainly the universe owed him something. Wasn't this, at least, the arithmetic of fairy tales? Girl loses parents, gains magical shape-shifting pumpkin, couture glass slippers, and prince. Why not: boy loses mother to cancer, acquires globally recognized sexual mastery? The anniversary of his mother's death had come and passed, but still he woke each morning listening for sounds of her—coffee brewing in the kitchen, her gold bangles clinking against a porcelain cereal bowl. What he needed was a bridge of adult bodily experiences to lead him away from the past, where his mother reigned with her brown sack lunches and grass-stained gardening gloves, and into his adulthood, where it would be all glass tumblers of whiskey and seedy midnight encounters with women in tight white T-shirts.

"It's between Roni and Sarah," he explained to his best friend, Andy. "But Sarah's the backup. I've been working on Roni for a few weeks now. She thinks we're going out."

They were out behind Temple Beth Emanuel, smoking a pack of Camels. Jett's secret was that he never inhaled all the way. He couldn't help but recall the overweight man who gave a lecture at their school the year before: the picture of the hole in his dead wife's throat, how Mr. Patton, the stoic history teacher, quietly gasped in the seat beside Jett. Jett never could tell if Andy actually inhaled the smoke; he hoped not.

It was Saturday morning and they were supposed to be at the post-service luncheon, but both boys had grown to hate the cold chopped liver and tuna sandwiches that were a staple of these events. Jett often wondered if there was a secret Jewish Food Emporium where all the old ladies shopped, the aisles stocked to the ceiling with stale thumb-print cookies and cheese sliced to the size of business cards.

"Roni, Roni, Roni," Andy said, and licked his lips. "My boy Jett's gonna eat him some Roni. Mac-a-Roni. Rice-a-Roni. A San Francisco treat, am I right?"

Jett stubbed out his cigarette. "We'll see," he said. "I'm going to her house tonight so I can help her with her English paper. She's a terrible writer."

"To be fair, the girl can barely speak English."

Roni was Israeli, which added to her sex appeal. She had dark skin. Dark hair. Dark eyes. There was a rumor that she routinely had phone sex with a paratrooper in the IDF.

Andy let a spiral of smoke out through his lips. "How are you gonna ask her?"

"You don't *ask* a girl to have sex. You just make the moves and it happens. It's about timing. And finesse."

"I don't know," Andy said. "I think you're supposed to ask. Have them sign a waiver or something."

"What do you know? You wouldn't know a vagina if one fell into your lap."

"At least *I've* been to second base. And where are you, Mr. Suave?" Andy made a visor with his hand, as if looking off into the distance. "Is that you out there, all the way on first? I think it is! And what are you up to out there? Is that your hand down your pants? It is!"

Jett was ready to knock the cigarette from Andy's mouth when Mrs. Kaczynski, their former Sunday school teacher, did it for him. "Cigarettes!" she said, standing before them, her bell-shaped frame erasing the sun. "And in the house of God!"

"Technically we're *outside* the house of God," Jett said. Where had she even come from? Perhaps God had dropped her from the sky.

Mrs. Kaczynski frowned. "I'm telling your mothers," she said, and then allowed, for the briefest moment, an apologetic smile. "Your father," she corrected herself. "I'm sorry, Jett, but I'll have to tell your father."

Andy looked visibly distressed; his parents were the spanking type. Jett's father operated on a higher level of punishment, one more cognitive than physical. He would revisit Jett's transgressions six months after the fact, when he could get the most use out of them. Like the time when Jett was ten and he accidentally killed his class gerbils, Cal Ripken Jr. and Cal Ripken Jr. Jr., after subjecting them to a tandem ride on his remote-control-operated U.S. Army fighter jet. Despite Jett's efforts to secure them with Scotch tape and rubber bands, the gerbils had fallen to what Jett hoped was a quick and painless death. His father, while upset at the time, did not punish Jett, saying only, "There are two things every man must do in his life: make mistakes and die." Jett buried the gerbils in a Life cereal box out back. It was his mother who murmured the mourner's Kaddish—the same Kaddish Jett and his father would recite not many years later as her casket descended into the earth. Jett's real punishment came a year after the gerbil incident, when he begged to keep one of the kittens that had taken up residence in their garage. It was then his dad recalled the gerbil incident and declared that Jett was forbidden from having pets until he was at least nineteen years old.

His mother had been the merciful one. It was she who would sneak into Jett's room after he'd done something bad—like pour chocolate milk into the fish tank, or run a magnet over the television—and smooth back his bangs, kiss him on the forehead. She would always love him. If he did a hundred and one bad things, she would forgive him a hundred and two times. He was her everything. Her baby.

But now all that was gone. Left was his father—his God. If Jett had been taught one thing, it was that there was no escaping God.

* * *

Roni had first seen Mr. Kaplan at Jett's bar mitzvah, which had taken place the day after she got her first period. It was a strange day, simultaneously triumphant and queasy. Her pad had bothered her during the service—it felt big and puffy, like a diaper—but she smiled each time she remembered it. As Jett droned on, singing his Torah portion in his nasally voice, she could only think one thing: she was a woman now—a woman! Of course Jewish tradition had, for thousands of years, denied women the opportunity to become daughters of the commandment—who needed a bat mitzvah when you had a period? Her blood was her bat mitzvah. Because of it, a new world was opening up before her, and Mr. Kaplan seemed a major player in it. He was a socialite—easily the most popular man in the congregation. After the service, he went around the temple like a politician, shaking the hands of the young and the old, kissing the foreheads of babies. He looked the part, with his slicked-back hair and three-piece suit, his demeanor softened by a sky blue kippah. While the other men—the old, liver-spotted Jews of Wichita—used the kippot to cover their bald spots (Roni sometimes wondered if they'd been invented just for that purpose), Jett's father wore the tiny silk headpiece like a crown. He was by far the most handsome man at the synagogue, a fact Roni recognized and appreciated even at twelve years old. Women flocked to him, pressing their hands to his chest or straightening his tie. Cynthia

Katz—president of the Mid-Kansas Jewish Federation—went so far as to wipe a bit of food from his cheek, saying, "Hold still, Aaron. You've got a bit of schmutzy." Later, Roni overheard Barbara Epstein-Hoffman say to Minnie Levy, "A man like that needs a woman. Just look at him. He's built for it." Minnie closed her eyes and nodded. "It's just a shame what happened to Melanie. And so young."

From that day on, Roni was saving herself for Mr. Kaplan. She asked her mother what he did, and her mother explained that he was in a business that turned other people's money into more money. Roni imagined Jett's father in a dark, candlelit room, turning nickels into diamonds with the wave of a hand. Eventually her crush became common knowledge among her friends. At sleepovers, when Roni slept with a pillow between her legs, her friends jokingly called the pillow Mr. Kaplan, asking if Mr. Kaplan enjoyed the view or if poor Mr. Kaplan could breathe under there. It was at one of these sleepovers that Roni's friend Whitney came up with the dare.

"You go to his house," Whitney said, "and you bring back a pair of his underwear."

The other girls broke out in a fit of disbelief. "It's just not even possible," someone said. "How's she supposed to get in his room?"

Whitney called for order and proposed a solution. "Obviously, she'll use Jett. You're friends with him, right?" She looked at Roni, whose hands were already trembling at the thought of Mr. Kaplan's underthings.

"He helps me with English homework," Roni said. "That's all."

"So you have an in," Whitney said. "Easy as pie."

"American pie," someone said, and everyone laughed, even Roni, who did not understand the joke. By this point, her crush had become its own point of satisfaction. It did not have to be Mr. Kaplan, she realized, but it did have to be a man. Not a boy—never a boy. A boy was too easy, too ordinary. And what did boys know about sex? Her fixation needed someone mature, someone who had been married, who had slept in a bed and made love so many times it was not a matter of keeping track in a diary. Someone who would know how to handle a girl. Daddy issues, the Americans would call it, but the Americans had a diagnosis for everything.

It was true that Roni's father was out of the picture, having remained in Tel Aviv, where he owned an insurance business and was dating a Russian immigrant named Galina. Upon moving in with Roni's father, Galina said her clothes smelled like Russia and demanded an entirely new wardrobe. She'd also convinced Roni's father to let her turn Roni's old bedroom into a combination yoga studio–craft room. If Roni ever went back to visit, she would have to sleep on the pullout sofa. Roni was supposed to talk to her father every Sunday at ten a.m. American time, but sometimes when she called, Galina would answer and say that her father was busy. "He's at the beach," she would say, although Roni's father had always hated the beach. He couldn't stand the feeling of sand between his toes.

Roni dreamed that Galina would die and that her father, in his grief, would ask Roni and her mother to return to Israel and live with him. He would convert the yoga studio back into her bedroom, returning their life to normal one piece of furniture at a time. But Galina seemed indestructible. Only a month before, she'd walked away from the scene of a car bombing with nothing but a small shrapnel wound above her eye.

* * *

As predicted, when Jett's father got the call from Ms. Kaczynski, he was not mad. He was *disappointed.* This was supposed to make Jett feel worse, but it didn't. Jett knew his father was still too distracted by grief to feel anything else, even anger, which was something like grief's first cousin. His father was stuck on a note: sad, sad, sad. He couldn't seem to reach any other register for even a moment, although Jett had tried to give him a nudge. Jett made jokes, acted out, got bad grades and then exceptional grades. Once, he purposefully spilled a bottle of Dr Pepper on a stack of his father's papers, just to see what would happen. His father had merely sighed and asked Jett to get some paper towels. At night, Jett could hear him weeping. It made him ache with something he'd never felt toward his father: contempt. If his father was going to cry, Jett at least wanted to be in on it. It frustrated Jett, who had cried all the time in the beginning. The tears had come on suddenly, out of nowhere, like a sneezing fit: in the frozen food isle, mid-push-up in gym class, while taking a bite of grilled cheese. Any little thing could remind him of his mother. Once, it was a can of stewed tomatoes. Another, the way one of his teachers scratched the skin beside her nose. He didn't mind. At school, he'd become a minor celebrity. Girls stared at him from across the cafeteria. The teachers let him turn in homework as late as he wanted. And then here was his dad, secreting his grief like it was a *Playboy*. Jett didn't like it at all.

On a sour note, he was still grounded.

"But I'm supposed to help Roni with her English paper," he said. "It's academic. Not social."

His father was making beans and weenies for dinner. This was the second night of beans and weenies that week; the night before had been Lucky Charms and instant mashed potatoes. Jett's mother had been the cook. His father was the businessman, the mathematician, the engineer. He could, if needed, unclog a toilet with a wire hanger, but boiling eggs was a conundrum. "Then Roni will have to come over here," his father said.

This was something Jett could work with. "All right, but just so you know, when I go over to Roni's house, her mom lets us study alone in her room. She even lets us close the door." Jett tried to keep his cool. "That's how we normally do it, and she'll expect it to go the same over here."

This didn't seem to faze his father, who was adding a pinch of sugar to the cauldron of Hebrew Nationals—his idea of a Michelin star meal. "Study on the moon for all I care," he said. "Just keep it down. I've got work to do."

Roni's mother dropped her off at dusk. She stood at Jett's front door in a white tank top and a pair of jean shorts. She held a red binder against her chest, the development of which Jett had been closely monitoring since the sixth grade, when she'd shown up at his bar mitzvah party in a sequined halter top.

"We don't have much time," Jett said. He took her by the arm and ushered her through the house and to his bedroom.

"Is your father home?" Roni asked.

"He's in his office."

"Can I meet him?"

Jett shut the door to his room and looked at his prize. "He's working."

"You know," she said, "all the girls have a crush on him."

"What?"

"All the girls at temple. He's handsome. Sammy says he looks like the hot uncle from a television show. I don't remember the name. *Full Home? Full Apartment?* Full something."

"He's an extremely busy man. And anyways, we need to get started on your paper."

Roni handed the binder to Jett. She sat on the floor and he sat on his bed. He was suddenly embarrassed by his bedspread, which was covered in a repeating pattern involving Buzz Lightyear and Woody the cowboy. He hadn't bothered to request a new one because why would he? Girls never came to his room. And besides, the bedspread had been a birthday present from his mother. Only wasteful, insecure people retired perfectly good bedspreads.

"Just so you know, this isn't my usual bedspread," he told Roni. "My usual one's in the wash. But this one, it's not that stupid, when you think about it. It's really soft, and the material's pretty good quality. And people would probably think you were mean if you joked about it."

Roni looked confused. "My grandmother back in Israel made my bedspread out of old baby clothes."

"That's really cultural of you," Jett said, and then turned back to her paper, which was, from what he could tell, complete nonsense. "This is a pretty good paper," he told her. "I'll just mark the grammar and spelling errors."

"I appreciate this," Roni said, and for one generous, billowing moment, she put her hand on his knee. She then leaned back so that she was resting on her elbows, her head tilted to the ceiling, where Jett had, years ago, meticulously arranged a galaxy of glow-in-the-dark stars according to a laminated star map his mother bought at the Cosmosphere gift shop. He made a mental note to take them down.

"Don't you just hate school?" Roni was saying. "Don't you wish you could live on the beach? In Israel, everywhere is a beach. You turn left and there's a beach. You turn right and there's a beach. Here it's just McDonald's and gas stations."

"We have wheat fields," Jett said. He hated when people talked about the ocean. He'd never been.

"Oh, wheat fields! Can you surf in them? Can you make castles or find seashells? No. Nobody does anything good in a wheat field. There's nothing fun here. I can't wait to graduate and move back to Israel."

"But you can't go back."

She looked at him. "Why not?"

"Because America's great. It's where the rest of the world wishes it could be."

She laughed at him. Not one of her usual shy giggles, but a full on laugh. A mean laugh. "No it's not. It's boring. One big giant yawn." She feigned a yawn for emphasis.

"We have fun here," Jett said. "Lots of fun."

"Doing what? Roping cows and eating pigs?"

"Let me show you," he said, and leaned in and kissed her on the mouth. He'd only kissed two other girls, but this time was clearly the best. Roni squirmed at first, but in time he found that her hand was on his leg, and then her tongue was searching his teeth. A thought flashed through his mind: *I, Jett Kaplan, am the greatest lover in the world.*

Eventually there developed an abundance of saliva that made Roni gag. They pulled apart and wiped their mouths and stared at each other like two strangers who had just witnessed the same plane crash.

Jett cleared his throat. "Would you like to do me a favor, Roni?"

"What is it?"

Jett looked down at his pants. He was wearing a pair of cargo shorts his mother had bought on clearance at Kohl's. He'd hated them at first, but now wore them often.

"You want me to do something with it?" she asked, gesturing toward his crotch.

He nodded, surprised by how easily she'd understood. "If you'd like to, why not?"

"I've never done it before," Roni said.

This was a lie. The whole freshman class knew that Roni had lost her virginity the year before, to an older guy at Camp B'nai B'rith. But perhaps she couldn't remember exactly how the act had transpired. As the story went, she'd had three whole bottles of Mike's Hard Lemonade.

"It'll be fun," Jett said. "That's what you want, right? Fun? *American fun?*"

She frowned. "Okay, but only if we can do it in your dad's room."

"What? Why not here? What's wrong with here?"

She looked at his bedspread and sighed.

Of course. *Toy Story*. What had his mother been thinking? It was something a five year old would have in his room. "If that's really what you want," he said. "But we have to be quiet."

They crept down the hall to the master bedroom. When his mother was alive, Jett and his parents used to watch movies in their bed. Jett would squeeze between the two of them or perch at the end, his bare feet kicking the air. Sometimes his mother would set a bowl of popcorn on his back. *Aaron, isn't it about time we get a new table? This one's tilted. And look—it's got such long hair. I do wish it would get a haircut.* Occasionally, if his father was in a good mood, he'd play along. *I'm not sure, Melanie. You know how expensive tables can be. And this one was such a steal. What are the chances we'll salvage another perfectly good table from a Dumpster fire?* Now, this kind of behavior was out of the question. Even memories of this nature were not allowed in the house after the funeral. Nothing, in fact, was allowed in the house after the funeral. Everything that had belonged to his mother—her Agatha Christie novels, her ceramic teapot with the cherry blossoms, her menorahs—all of it was donated to Jett's aunt Esther. All that remained was a thin orange cardigan that hung, inexplicably, from the back of a chair in the dining room. "It's better this way," his father had assured him. And perhaps it was. Jett dreaded the day he would visit his aunt Esther's house—the avalanche of his mother, one coffee mug at a time.

When he opened the door to his father's room, Jett was surprised to find it exactly as he remembered. He figured his father would have done a complete overhaul—rearranged the furniture, hung new curtains, put out new bedding. But the room was untouched. It even smelled of her, like cinnamon candles and peach shampoo. There was her hairbrush on the bureau. There was her hair.

"Do you mind if I go to the bathroom?" Roni was asking. "To freshen up?"

Women were always saying this in movies, and Jett hated them for it. When did a man ever ask to freshen up? Why couldn't someone just be naturally fresh? Further, Jett didn't like the idea of her in his mother's bathroom. But what could he do? He told her to go ahead and watched as she went into the bathroom—the bathroom with the Jacuzzi tub his mom once filled with oatmeal when he had the chickenpox—and shut the door.

* * *

Roni smiled to herself in the mirror. She was in Mr. Kaplan's bathroom, and so far, she hadn't had to do anything too unsavory to get there. She was sure Jett would expect something of her soon enough, but she would deal with him when the time came. Now, she focused her attention on the bathroom. It was a big bathroom, equipped with what her mother called a bubble tub. The washroom led into a dark, cedar closet. The left side clearly belonged to Jett's father, whose shirts hung like a procession of deflated cotton ghosts. Everything was tidy, down to the row of leather shoes beneath the shirts, in the place where the ghosts' feet would have gone. And then there was the other side of the closet, the side that had belonged to Jett's mother. Her clothes were everywhere—balled up on the floor, half-hanging from hangers, erupting from a plastic laundry basket. At the far end hung a white dress covered in a million translucent beads, like fish eggs. Roni opened the top drawer of the dresser and found that it too was separated. On the left was a row of Mr. Kaplan's neatly folded boxer briefs. On the right, a haphazard assortment of panties: silk, cotton, lace. Buried among them was a small white tube. Thinking it was lotion, Roni undid the crusted cap and brought the tube to her nose. The smell was awful, like medicine. She looked at the label. VAGINAL ITCH RELIEF CREAM. Roni replaced the tube and put it back in the drawer. How sad, she thought. A dead woman's itch cream.

"Roni?" Jett called from the bedroom.

"Just a second," she said, and quickly grabbed the first pair of Mr. Kaplan's underwear she could find—a pair of navy blue briefs. Having nowhere else to put them, she stuffed them into her shorts, down the backside.

Jett was lying on the bed, belly-up, with his hands crossed over his chest. When she came out he sat up onto his elbows and smiled at her. "Hey," he said.

"Hey," she said back, and took a small step toward the bed, hoping he wouldn't notice the lump in the seat of her shorts.

"Come here, you," Jett said, and patted the empty space next to him. She went over and he was immediately on her, kissing her. "Are you ready?" he asked, gesturing to the sad bulge in his pants.

"I won't go all the way," Roni said, "but I can use my hands."

Within seconds he'd pulled his pants down to his knees. Roni tried not to appear disgusted. She focused her mind on Mr. Kaplan's underwear—her victory prize. After a series of awkward maneuvers, she began to inflict on Jett what she hoped would be the coldest, driest hand job of his life. After a few disturbing moments, the thing had gone nearly limp inside her hands. Naked mole rat, she thought. Baby naked mole rat.

"Why isn't anything happening?" she asked, playing dumb.

"Can you spit on it maybe? That would help."

"You spit on it," she told him. "It's your penis."

He shrugged, as if seeing her point. He grabbed her hand and hawked a wad of spit onto her palm.

Even the neighbors must have heard her scream. "Pig!" she cried. "American pig!" She was about to wipe the spit onto the bed, but before she could execute the move, Jett's father burst through the door.

For a moment, Mr. Kaplan stood in the doorway, examining the tableau before him. Jett's pants were still half off and Roni's hand was clenched around the wad of saliva. Mr. Kaplan looked at Jett and then looked down at his own feet. "I always figured your mother would deal with this kind of thing."

Roni rushed to her feet, and it was then that the underwear fell from her shorts. They lay on the floor like a landmine, daring for someone to move.

"What is that?" Jett asked, pointing to the heap of fabric.

Jett's father stooped down and plucked the garment from the earth. He rubbed the cotton between his fingers. Only now did Roni see the little white bow—a feminine bow—stitched to the waistband.

"I think it's time you go home," Mr. Kaplan said.

* * *

Jett sat with Roni while they waited for her mother to arrive. His father had gone straight to the kitchen, where he was now reheating leftover beans and weenies on the stove. He often did this—had a second go at dinner rather than expend the effort of making dessert. It was Jett's mother who had so thoroughly covered sundaes with chopped walnuts, sliced strawberries, and caramel syrup that you could no longer tell what flavor ice cream you were eating. Jett watched from the couch in the living room as his father absentmindedly stirred the corpse of their dinner, trying to revive it.

"Hey," Roni said, placing a warm hand on Jett's knee. She would not meet his eyes. "I don't know if I ever told you, but I'm really sorry about your mom."

Jett sat back, nodding as her hand began to run lovingly up and down his thigh. He noticed the lack of interest in his pants. Instead, a stinging sensation was building behind his eyes and a knot tied and retied itself in his throat. Roni's hand kept on, sliding up and down his leg, occasionally squeezing his knee. He closed his eyes and let himself imagine that it was not Roni's hand but his mother's. He pictured her long fingers, the nails painted with a clear, bitter-tasting polish meant to keep her from biting them. He would open his eyes and there she would be, at last, smiling at him—the familiar mole above her left eyebrow, the smell of her perfume wafting from her orange cardigan. She would laugh about what had happened with Roni. "Don't worry," she would tell him. "It'll make a great story one day. Just wait and see." And then she would get up, smooth her cotton skirt, and kiss him on the top of his head, her gold Star of David necklace bumping against his nose. She would go check on his father, that old lump. He never could be trusted in the kitchen. Remember the time he put salt in everyone's cocoa? Or when he stuck a whole corncob down the disposal? Undoubtedly, he was causing a scene at the stove. Probably burning the hotdogs, like always.

Queen of England

Dewy and I were not good sons. At home, we sliced the drapes to make togas and blasted birds with pellet guns we weren't supposed to have. To make our mother nervous, we pressed our skulls to the microwave door and licked the sticky bottoms of our sneakers. At the grocery store, we fondled bananas and played catch with bags of rice that always, to her horror, broke open in a grand display of her poor parenting. Sometimes, if we were especially bored, we slipped notes into strangers' palms that read: "HELP US, WE'VE BEEN KID-NAPPED!" Everywhere we went, people looked at our mother as if she were trapped in a cage with a pair of rabid hyenas. In return, she treated us like princes. She had nobody else to love.

She was a small woman, topping out at five feet on a good day, and often complained that she did not have more hands than children. Our father fled when I was just a bun in the oven—to do what, we were never told. I guessed piracy, but Dewy told me it probably involved another woman or vodka or maybe both. I preferred my version, picturing him with a peg leg and an eye patch. My greatest hope was that he'd return to Wichita with a colossal black beard and a treasure chest full of gold and put us up in one of the mansions out by the racquet club. We'd crank the heat in the winter and the AC in the summer, name-brand turkey would appear in our lunchboxes. Dewy said I might as well sit around and wait for Jesus.

Dewy was two years older, but by the time I was eleven and he thirteen, I was already a head taller and working on a mustache.

None of this mattered, because Dewy was light-years sharper, and it was understood that my growing older would do nothing to close the gap. It wasn't that he was a genius—he was smart, though nothing to alert the news about—but that he had a politician's combination of grit and cunning. He was constantly sharpening his senses to prepare for the more generous world he was certain awaited him outside of our mother's house. He studied chess and electrical engineering and said things like *indubitably* just to be an asshole. In his free time, he taught himself Portuguese and Morse code, memorized the name of every capital city in the Western Hemisphere. Meanwhile, I was a pain in the public school system's thigh, or so a janitor once told me. Whatever hope my mother had for her progeny resided wholly and completely in Dewy. And so when our mother began bringing home men, Dewy took it worse than I did—he had more to lose. He understood that our mother was a limited commodity, and that any time and energy spent on a man was less time and energy spent on him.

The men were all the same—short, lecherous creatures with halos of hair and greasy skin. Most were from Kansas City and had at least one fat wife under their belts. Dewy hated each one more than the last. He put thumbtacks in their loafers and accused them, without any rationale, of being Nazis. "Heil Hitler?" he would say to them in passing.

Most didn't last more than two dates.

Despite Dewy's efforts, our mother eventually attached herself to one of these men, and it was like watching a swan eat a cigarette butt. I'd seen this once, during a field trip to the botanical gardens, when Miss Robertson flicked her cigarette into the bird pond.

This was all at the beginning of summer break, when Dewy and I had no time for new enemies. There were rocket ships to build and neighbor girls to terrify. And yet there he was—in our house, at our dinner table, his massive hands slithering all over our mother's body.

His name was Walter McDonald, but we took to calling him the Weenie. His skin was the color and texture of a cooked hotdog and, on most nights, he came to dinner smelling of Canadian bacon. He owned a chain of pizza parlors, and it was with this money—this pizza money—that he purchased our mother's affection. Within weeks, objects began to materialize around the house: a television, a set of aerating wine glasses, a shiny red KitchenAid. On our mother's slender neck, a string of pearls the size of baby teeth. Her wardrobe transformed and she became the type of woman who wore silk blouses with opalescent snaps instead of T-shirts that advertised national parks she'd never been to. "Isn't your mom a looker?" the Weenie would say before covering her with a barrage of kisses.

He gave Dewy and me our own offerings—boyish trinkets like baseball cards and Pogs—but it wasn't enough to negate the fact that at night we could hear him groaning away like a lawnmower in our mother's bedroom.

One night, Dewy and I were in the kitchen microwaving a troll doll when we heard our mother cry out, "Just *do* it already, cowboy king!" And then, a wave of laughter.

"I'll kill him," Dewy said, clenching his fists. "I'll sneak in there while he's sleeping and I'll cut off his hands."

"His feet, too," I said, although my heart wasn't in it. I had, at some point, grown fond of the Weenie. I didn't understand it, since I too cringed each time he put an eye on our mother, but there was something comforting about his salmon-colored shirts, the smell of his Polo aftershave. Even the sight of his leather shoes in the hallway produced an aura of safety. I knew it would have to remain my secret—my own little bundle of pleasures. Dewy could never know that I borrowed the Weenie's Old Spice deodorant, or that I liked to watch him tie his tie in the mornings, his thick fingers working the silky material. Or that I found a peculiar gratification in the sounds coming from our mother's bedroom. That on some nights I would lie motionless in bed, listening for them. Summoning them.

One afternoon, after our mother had already fallen in love, the Weenie decided that Dewy and I needed a tree fort. "Every boy should have a tree fort," he said, and rushed off to the hardware store to gather the necessities.

Dewy saw the fort as a mixed blessing. The Weenie was giving us something we could use—a place to call our own—but this privacy would come at a cost. For as long as the weather was good, we would be expected to occupy our station outside, away from our mother. Away from the Weenie. We could hear it already. *Walter builds you a great big fort and all you want to do is sit inside and watch TV?* It was a minor victory, but Dewy was going to let him have it.

In terms of actually building the fort, Dewy and I assumed the Weenie would do the hands-on work while we participated in some peripheral way, perhaps by bringing him water or offering verbal encouragements. But the Weenie soon had us sawing wood and hammering nails. I caught on relatively quickly, but Dewy immediately spilled a case of nails and managed a splinter the size of a toothpick. A rash on his forearms suggested an allergy to wood.

"What kind of boy's allergic to wood?" the Weenie asked, winking at me.

Suddenly, Dewy was screaming. When we looked over, he was clutching his hand to his chest. Dark blood pooled on his shirt.

"Goddamn it," the Weenie said, rushing over. "What'd you do now?"

"The saw slipped. Maybe if you'd taught me how to use it right."

Soon Mom was outside, chanting, "What's happened? What's happened?"

"Quiet," the Weenie told her. He wrapped the wound in a towel and led Dewy to his truck. Throughout the process, he kept calling Dewy a moron. *A goddamned moron with mush for brains.* Dewy, who at the age of eleven rewired the lights so that when our mother turned on the oven, the radio would tune to her favorite oldies station. He was now a moron. A *goddamned moron.* Part of me was thrilled to hear it.

After the hospital, we sat down for dinner as if nothing had happened. Mom was too frazzled to cook, so she put a frozen lasagna in the microwave and gave us each a cup of fruit cocktail—the good kind, with grape halves and maraschino cherries. We were silent except for the Weenie, who thought it an appropriate time to regale us with stories of his father's heroics. His father had gotten his ear blown off in the trenches of Normandy. His father had pulled a little girl out of a house fire by the ponytail. His father had once sailed from Florida to Cuba on a boat made from old apple crates. This, he seemed to be saying, was the kind of manhood boys like us would never achieve.

Meanwhile, Dewy refused to eat. The tip of his right thumb was gone, lost somewhere in the yard. On the way back from the hospital, the Weenie had explained that if we didn't want to continue helping with the fort then we didn't deserve to have one in the first place. He'd use the extra wood to build our mother a garden bed, and that would be that.

Our mother had nothing to say about any of it. She ate her dinner and then carried our dirty dishes to the sink. All the while, the Weenie watched her movements, a predator tracking his prey. When the dishes were done, he led her into her bedroom. It was not even dark before Dewy and I could hear his growls, our mother's whimpers. Like something being eaten alive.

The Fourth of July came and went, leaving a bad taste in everyone's mouth. There was an incident involving a Roman candle and a catapult Dewy and I fashioned from the fort scraps. I wanted to forget about it—to move on—but the Weenie now had a scar above his lip, and every night we had to watch as our mother rubbed tea tree oil onto the wound.

By now the Weenie understood that Dewy and I were not normal children, and that ours was not a normal household. "You do know you're the parent, right?" he'd tell our mother. "You own them. You *made* them."

Our mother could only shrug and tell him that she'd tried. It had been hard, raising us alone. She had done her best.

"That's fine, but I'm here now," he told her. "Let me do my best."

Not a day later, Dewy took the Weenie's wallet, inside of which he discovered a picture of a woman—a pink-faced, double-chinned creature with a crown of orange hair. Who the woman was, we didn't know, but Dewy cut out her face, which he proceeded to paste onto a picture of a piggy bank. He then taped his project to the refrigerator and waited.

"They were in my things," the Weenie told our mother when he saw it. "They were in my things and they violated my private property. I can't prove it, but I'm sure they took some money, too."

Dewy and I listened from the living room.

"I'm sorry," our mother said. "But they're boys. They just do these things sometimes."

"That's the whole point—they're just boys. And they need a good straightening out so they don't grow up to be bad men. This is how criminals are born."

Our mother appeared in the living room, where Dewy and I had been etching our gangster names into her beloved coffee table. We called it the coffin table, because it was so ugly it belonged underground. Our mother had made it the summer before, during a brief but intolerable crafting phase in which the house smelled continuously of paint and we all went to bed each night with a headache. She'd painted the table a sunset orange, but the paint was now peeling, and chips of it would turn up in our bed sheets and snow boots and, once, the center of a roast beef sandwich she'd packed me for lunch. She claimed to love the table more than anything else in the house, although perhaps deep down she knew it was a failure. She had not made anything since.

"Which one of you did it?" she asked.

Dewy and I looked at each other.

"If one of you doesn't fess up, I'll have to assume you're both guilty."

Dewy looked at me. He knew I wouldn't betray him.

"Fine," she said. "Then you're both grounded."

"Grounded?" Dewy asked. "What are we, a fifties sitcom?"

"Don't start with me," she said, and then left to report back to the Weenie.

I glared at Dewy. "You could have told her I didn't do it."

"We can't have them pitting us against one another. We're stronger together."

I said nothing and continued to carve my name into the table. I wanted to tell the Weenie that I hadn't been a part of it. That this time, I was the good kid, and that I might, with the proper forces, grow up to be a good man, just like his father and his father's father and all the other men who came before him.

And then suddenly he was there, in the living room, charging toward us. He grabbed Dewy by the underarms and, with one fluid motion, threw him onto the couch, facedown. Before Dewy could struggle, the Weenie yanked down his pants and administered exactly five sharp slaps to the pale flesh of Dewy's behind.

"Walter, be gentle" was all our mother could say, and this in barely a whisper. She was standing in the corner, her fingernails in her mouth.

Dewy's mouth unhinged into a silent scream. He was determined not to yell, but where his mouth could obey, his body could not. The moment the Weenie finished, Dewy let out a fart—high and long and clear as a birdsong. From the corner, our mother began to laugh. She clapped a hand over her mouth. Dewy looked at her and narrowed his eyes.

The Weenie then turned to me. "Are you scared?" he asked.

I shook my head.

"That's because you didn't do it. Dewy did it. Is that right?"

I didn't dare move. Dewy sat on the couch, watching, his face pale and mottled.

"All right, then. If you're not willing to talk." He did not grab me as he had Dewy, but instead led me to the couch and let me position myself on the cushions. The sound of the spanking, of his hand meeting my skin, belied the fact that it did not hurt—he was not trying.

The next day, Dewy began making threats. "The next time the Weenie stays the night, I'm ripping up my homework," he told our mother.

"Don't be dramatic," she said. "It's summer." We were in the car, on the way to a restaurant where the Weenie had reservations. Dewy had gel in his hair and she'd made us wear stiff button-down shirts with horses on the breast pockets—presents from the Weenie.

"Then I'll take his wallet again. And this time I'll burn it."

"Why can't you just let me be happy for once?" she asked.

"Don't *we* make you happy?"

"You make me happy in a different way. And I deserve to be completely happy. Don't you think I deserve that?"

"Your logic is skewed," Dewy explained, putting on his scholarly voice. "As a mother, you're obligated to pursue a happiness that makes your children happy, too. But you want the Weenie around for yourself. For the company and the fun and—let's not kid ourselves—his money. You want his money, and that's selfish. And mothers should never be selfish. It's not in their evolutionary nature."

"Dewy," she said, her knuckles white on the steering wheel. "Have you ever thought that if you talked like a boy for once you might have a few more friends besides your brother?" She turned to look at him. "Nobody likes a smart-ass."

Dewy turned to the road and stared.

At the restaurant, he refused to speak. When the waiter came around, he simply pointed to the menu.

"We had a little tiff in the car," our mother explained to the Weenie.

The Weenie chuckled. "I once gave my parents the silent treatment for a whole week. It'll pass. Isn't that right, Dewy? Eventually you'll need something and you'll have to speak?"

Dewy did not seem to register this question, or any other stimuli. I knew his new minimum of silence was a week. If Dewy knew one thing, it was discipline. He'd once eaten nothing but foods with blue dye for a whole month, to see if it would change the color of his stools. He'd marked his data in a spiral notebook, which he kept on top of the toilet. In the end, he'd developed stomach cramps and his tongue grew a white film that he had to scrape off into the sink each night. Our mother nearly died of worry—she took to dissolving vitamins in his blueberry Kool-Aid, so he wouldn't get scurvy.

The Weenie became Dewy's greatest antagonist. "Hey, Dewy," he'd say, giving Dewy a soft punch on the shoulder. "How about a sing-along? *She'll be coming around the mountain when she comes . . .*"

Our mother would laugh at this, a reaction that only solidified Dewy's determination.

In the meantime, I was the one who suffered most. Mom and the Weenie had each other, and Dewy had his own imagination, but I had nobody and nothing. Because of Dewy, I'd made little effort with the boys in my own grade. As a result, they thought I was a jerk. Maybe they assumed I thought I was better than them, but they would have been wrong. It was Dewy who was better than them. What kid my age could build a rocket out of pop cans, or properly dissect a dead pigeon so as to remove the tiny heart unscathed? While they were playing basketball and dreaming of sports cars, Dewy was intercepting police radio waves and fine-tuning his hot-wiring skills. We had a dream to steal Mom's station wagon and drive until we reached an ocean. We'd never been outside of Kansas and liked to muse about what awaited us past the state line: mountains and deserts and cities with skyscrapers. Dewy had a plan to work for the FBI in Washington, D.C., while I made big money fishing salmon in Alaska. Now, even a tiny adventure seemed unlikely. Dewy would barely look at me.

He broke his silence only once. It was early in his protest, and we were sitting together on the back porch. Mom had given us half of a watermelon to share, and we were hauling out the pink meat with an ice cream scoop. She and the Weenie had gone inside, to take showers.

"Why didn't you go silent with me?" Dewy asked.

I put down the scoop and stared at him. "You're talking."

"I want to know why you didn't go silent with me. I thought we were in this together—like with the wallet. Didn't you hear what Mom said? About us not having friends?"

"She said *you* didn't have any friends."

"She meant the both of us," he said. "It's always the both of us."

I looked at him, at his chapped lips and the dark pimples that had begun to appear on his jaw line. I wondered, for the first time, if he might not grow up to be good-looking. "Maybe I don't want to do everything you do," I said. "Maybe I don't want everyone to hate me." I waited for a speech—something eloquent and mean and convincing—but there was only the sound of a distant lawn mower.

"Give me this," he finally said, and wrenched the ice cream scoop from my hand. He ate the rest of the melon on his own.

Everyone was nervous for Dewy's birthday. It fell on a Sunday, which meant that Mom and the Weenie were already out of the house when Dewy and I woke up. The Weenie had somehow convinced our mother to go to church with him, a ritual Dewy and I considered blasphemous. Dewy had long ago converted me to atheism, and so it was painful to think of our mother dressed in some ridiculous outfit, kneeling and singing among lunatics. And yet, we'd come to enjoy having the house to ourselves on Sunday mornings. We'd eat whatever we could find for breakfast—cookies, whipped cream, string cheese—and then position ourselves in front of the new television like monks before an altar. Occasionally we'd go through Mom's room, searching for things to steal or destroy. Otherwise, we took it easy, pretending we'd landed in some alternate universe where children were masters over the adults.

I figured Dewy would be especially excited because it was his birthday, that maybe he would talk to me again. I found him sitting at the kitchen table, reading the newspaper.

"Happy birthday," I told him.

For a moment, he forgot himself and smiled. I realized, suddenly, how much I missed him: missed talking to him, listening to him, learning from him. I wondered, for the first time, if the distance between us might remain even if he did start talking again.

Before I could say anything else, Mom and the Weenie came through the door. The Weenie was holding a large white cake, which he brought to the table and set before Dewy.

"Happy birthday, sweetie," Mom said, and kissed him on the crown of his head.

Dewy stared at the cake, as if he expected it to speak for him. Mom went ahead and lit the candles, and on her command, we started to sing. Dewy's face puckered and paled. At the end of the song, we all held our breath, waiting to see if he would blow the candles. He inhaled, as if preparing for it, and then, without fanfare, hocked a gigantic loogie onto the center of the cake. There was something green inside of it, maybe a fleck of lettuce. More than ever before, I was in awe of him. My brother.

"You little shit," the Weenie said, and slapped the kitchen table so that the cake rattled and the loogie shook back and forth on the frosting. "You're going to eat this cake. You hear me?"

None of this fazed Dewy, who did not so much as blink.

The Weenie then grabbed Dewy's hand—the dirty bandage still on the thumb—and plunged it into the cake, whose candles were still flickering. He then brought the cakey hand to Dewy's mouth. All the while, Mom politely requested that he stop. "Stop it, Walter," she kept saying, as if he were simply tickling the back of her neck. The Weenie continued, bringing Dewy's hand from the cake to his mouth. Cake to mouth. Cake to mouth. "Eat it," he said. "Goddamn it, you'll eat this cake." Dewy's eyes soon disappeared behind a mask of white frosting. A whimper escaped his mouth.

I was not yet a large boy, but the force of my fists on the Weenie's belly was enough to break his spell. He let go of Dewy and took me by the wrists, his thumbs digging into my skin. "Who do you think you are?" he asked, his face inches from my own. Frosting dotted his chin. "You two worthless shits don't deserve the half of your mother. Do you know that? The poor angel. Stuck here with you little creeps. And what do you do? Tell me. What do you do to deserve this roof over your head?"

He expected an answer, but he was hurting my wrists and all I could do was look at my mother, to gauge her reaction to see whom she loved more: me or the Weenie. But she was not looking at either of us; she was busy cleaning the cake from Dewy's face with a paper napkin. "It's all right," she whispered to him. "It'll be all right." Ever so slightly, Dewy nodded. Snot was running down his nose, carving through the frosting above his lip.

I turned back to the Weenie. "I'm sorry, sir," I told him. I had never called him sir before, but I couldn't help it. I wanted, more than anything, to be somebody's favorite.

And then, Dewy's voice. "Don't apologize," he said. "Not to *him*."

The Weenie let go of my wrists. "And there it is. There's the big man with the big voice. How about you use that big boy voice to say thank you? Can you say it? Say, *Thank you for the birthday cake, Mom.*"

Dewy glared at him through his mask of frosting. "I'll say thank you once you stop fucking my mother."

Everyone went silent. Mom stood above Dewy, the napkin still in hand. I could hear the Weenie breathing—the quiet tick of his wrist-watch. And then he was gathering his things: keys, Thermos, the leather briefcase he was never without. He went to stand near my mother, whose chest was moving up and down, up and down. She closed her eyes and we all prepared for him to kiss her good-bye. Instead, he lifted his arms and, without even touching her skin, unclasped the pearl necklace, which he slipped easily into his breast pocket.

He cleared his throat and leaned toward Dewy. "Buddy, I wouldn't fuck the Queen of England if it meant I had to put up with you for even one more day."

And then he left.

Our mother took to her bedroom and stayed there through the night—there was no further mention of Dewy's birthday. When she came out in the morning, she floated down the hallway and into the kitchen, her eyes swollen and pink. She did not say anything but simply placed food onto the table and then removed it when we were finished. She took out the trash and brought in the mail and other-wise performed all of her motherly duties, but she did not look us in the eyes and she did not speak to us. She was like a robot version of herself—Dewy dubbed her AutoMom.

I wanted to do something—hug her or tell her she looked pretty—but I worried it would have no effect. It was one thing to know I could make her miserable; it was another to know I could not make her happy. And so I simply watched as she moved through hallway after hallway of the sadness we had built for her, finding not a single door out.

During those days, the Queen of England appeared in my mind often. I was surprised to find her there, an image of white hair and gold jewelry. I began to repeat the Weenie's words, testing out dif-ferent inflections. Fuck the Queen of *England. Fuck* the *Queen* of

England. I could not determine why he'd chosen her, this emblem of royalty. Did he mean her as she was in her present state—old and wrinkled and surely at the end of her power? Or as she was in her youth—a princess on the brink of authority? Did people even consider her beautiful? Among the pool of celebrities and supermodels, she seemed a bizarre choice. I'd learned about other queens in my history classes, and from what I could tell, most were not standards of beauty. They stared out from the textbook with sharp, brooding eyes and pinched little mouths. They had petite, heart-shaped heads that poked up from ridiculous outfits. Each appeared more constipated than the last. So what exactly had the Weenie been saying to us, to our mother? How exactly did he think she compared to the Queen?

Perhaps the question was also tormenting our mother, because an entire week passed before she spoke to us again. We were sitting in the living room. Dewy was reading volume two of the *Encyclopedia Britannica.* I was striking and then blowing out matches, trying to get the house to smell like a campfire. Mom was cross-legged on the floor, writing a letter—to whom, we'll never know. She didn't often write letters, but it was something she took up on occasion, like baking bread or rearranging the furniture. There'd been times like this before, days when she retreated into the privacy of her mind and we'd have to say her name four or five times in a row—*Mom, Mom, Mom, Mom, Mom*—in order to get a response. But this time was different. This time, she'd gone somewhere deeper, somewhere we couldn't reach. She put down her pen and ran a finger across the coffin table, where Dewy and I had sketched our names. She looked up at us, as if struck by an idea.

"Have I been a good mother?" she asked.

Dewy and I stopped what we were doing. I could see that Dewy was preparing an analysis of exactly how, according to Western science and history and philosophy, she had failed us, and so I said, "Yes. You've been the best." I knew it was not completely true—she had, after all, brought the Weenie into our lives, and for this, Dewy would never forgive her, which meant that I too could never forgive her. At least not fully. But who was I to kick her when she was already down? Who was I to be greedy with my love? I'd learned at least this much.

Bald Bear

It was understood that Maxine and I were waiting for men. It was the dead center of July and the Kansas sun was poised like the face of a hammer ready to strike. In the lake, diapers surfaced jellyfish style, and children war painted with sunscreen pressed bottle caps to their ears, listening for an ocean they'd likely never seen. Maxine and I started rubbing sunscreen onto each other; there was nothing sorority girl about it. For the type of girls we were—both from hearty, Irish stock, our bodies like two peeled potatoes—the application of sunscreen was more of a medical procedure than anything else.

Maxine was working on my shoulders when a pair of men appeared before us, one holding a fishing pole, the other a hotdog. We were familiar with their kind: late-twenty-somethings who wore cutoffs and toted red Playmate coolers filled with Hamm's. They came to the lake to drink and fish and sneak glances at girls in bikinis. The fisherman's fly was down, and he was severely sunburned on his cheeks and nose, as if someone had taken a frying pan to his face. The hotdog eater was better: tall and tanned with a lumberjack beard. He was attractive—genuinely attractive—and seemed completely unaware of it.

"How we doing, ladies?" the fisherman asked, speaking through a cheek of chew. Either something blew into the hotdog eater's eye, or he winked at me.

"Perfectly fine," I said, half wanting them to go away. I could foresee the whole thing: the hotdog eater would go for Maxine, who was objectively prettier and funnier than me, and I'd be stuck with the fisherman. "Can we help you?"

"We just wanted to come by and invite you to a barbecue," the fisherman said. He tilted his head toward the parking lot, where a group of people were gathered around a charcoal grill.

I was hungry and bored and had a deep love for barbecues, but I wasn't about to accept an invitation from strangers. Luckily, Maxine had an inherent affection for strangers—yet another quality that drew men to her. She once drove all the way to Aspen with a guy she met in a yoga class. She invited me along but I told her we'd both end up dead in a ditch. As it turned out, the guy was related to a famous screenwriter and the three of them—Maxine, the guy, the screenwriter—spent the weekend drinking cognac in an outdoor hot tub. She hadn't even had to kiss anyone. "Actually, I'm starving," she told the fisherman, and began to gather her things. She looked at me, eyebrows raised. "You coming?"

Not wanting to be alone, I put on most of my clothes and followed her to the parking lot.

In our defense, we had not come to Clinton Lake to meet men but to escape my apartment, which was filled with poison. I'd fallen victim to a rather bad flea infestation and, after weeks of scratching and telling myself they'd eventually go away, I'd caved and set off a bug bomb. Before leaving my apartment, I watched as the metal canister released a cloud of toxic white fog. There was something pretty about it—an amorphous poison genie slithering from its lamp. Safe at the lake, I dreaded going back home, where I would have to clean every surface with a hot washrag, as well as wash any clothes, bedding, dishes, and towels that may have come in contact with the fog. Even the doorknobs would be coated in poison.

Worse than the fleas was that I didn't own an animal. It seemed an injustice, like a born-again virgin getting struck down by an STD. The fleas had come from the cat of an art history professor who was twice my age and who, as soon as I mentioned meeting his parents, slipped away by such tiny increments that I was suddenly shocked to find myself single. One day he was there—his books on the coffee table, his brown bottle of men's thickening shampoo in the shower—and the next he was gone, leaving behind nothing but a sea of invisible flea eggs, courtesy of the overweight, walleyed calico he often brought over because he couldn't bear the thought of her sleeping alone.

Exactly two days after he left, the fleas exploded in a grand display of evolutionary fine-tuning. They jumped in great arcs from the carpet and left itchy pink bites along my ankles and thighs. In the mornings, I woke with wild streaks of blood across my sheets, from where I'd clawed myself in my sleep. "Look at me, I made a Jackson Pollock," I whispered one morning. There was nobody there to hear me.

The barbecue offered scratchy country music from a boom box and a few folding chairs, the kind with thick strips of plastic that stick to your skin. In time, we were all introduced. The fisherman's name was Walt. The hotdog eater was Jackson. Maxine introduced herself and explained that we were coworkers at the university's admissions office, where we spent our days talking to potential students or, more often, their parents. Neither of us liked our job, but we had nothing else in the way of skills or interests. The only thing we'd accomplished was college itself—it made sense that we'd turn around and peddle it to others.

Surprisingly, Maxine took an interest in Walt, who was not as chubby as he'd originally appeared and who looked rather handsome in a baseball cap and aviators. She usually went for the lanky, artistic type—men who made their living painting murals or assembling sequined finger puppets for the arts center. She admitted to liking men who were interesting, not because she liked interesting men, but because dating interesting men made her feel interesting by proximity. While Maxine and Walt talked, Jackson let his hand hover over my lower back and attended to my cup of beer. I was giddy as he delivered paper plates loaded with warm strawberries and sweaty cheese cubes the color of duck feet. When he tried to feed me buffalo wings I told him I was a vegetarian. He looked at me as if I'd confessed to something shameful, like a case of chlamydia or an affinity for hair bands. It was a look I knew well. My mother had given it to me when I first told her I was giving up meat. "But, darling," she'd said, "vegetarian households always smell like pee."

Before long, Maxine and Walt came up to Jackson and me. "We're going back to town," Maxine said, grabbing at Walt's hand. "You guys need a ride?"

"I've got my truck," Jackson offered. "I can take us back in a little bit." He looked at me for approval. Part of me wanted to stick to the original plan, which was to get ice cream sandwiches and watch a horror movie at Maxine's place. But Maxine looked so excited and Jackson smelled like something familiar, maybe pine trees or rain, and so I said okay.

Jackson drove a tan pickup. I sat in the passenger seat with a six-pack of warm Coors at my feet and a tackle box on my lap. From the rearview mirror dangled a red air freshener in the shape of a naked lady, the word CINNAMON stamped in cursive across her breasts.

"So you're some sort of scholar, is that right?" Jackson asked. We were on a highway going what was probably too fast.

"Not exactly," I said. "It's more like sales than anything else. It's just I sell college instead of snake oil."

"Still, you're on campus all day. Makes you something of an academic."

"My mother would love to hear you say that," I said, and then immediately panicked. Why had I mentioned my mother? Men hated when you mentioned parents. If they had their way, every woman would be an orphan. I pressed my hand to the vent—hot air was coming out. "So what do you do?" I asked, trying to change the subject.

"Fish. Hunt."

"I mean, for work."

"That's right."

I realized he was not the type to joke about matters of fishing or hunting. "You can live off that?"

"Sure—between meat and furs. I make all kinds of stuff from furs. And skins. If you make something, rest assured there's some kook out there who'll buy it. Learned that from the Internet. One time I made a doll out of horse hair. Just a little doll with pearl button eyes and a burlap dress. Some lady bought it off eBay for a hundred bucks. Said she only gave her baby organic, handcrafted toys. Can you even imagine a baby snuggling with a horsehair doll?"

"I had no idea there was a market for that kind of thing."

"If you build it, they will come."

Jackson turned off the air and cranked down the windows. Usually I didn't like driving with the windows down—the wind tangled my hair and bothered my contacts. But in the truck I hung an arm out, feeling the invisible grooves in the air.

I'd gotten used to telling myself I didn't want a man. My mother had summed it up the last time I called her crying about the ex: it was time for me to be alone, to be a single and independent woman with a bachelor's degree and a one bedroom. I needed to learn to like myself, to enjoy my own company—something my mother feared she had never done. At least this was what I reminded myself as Jackson pulled up in front of my apartment.

He was looking at me, his car idling. "This is it, right?"

By now, enough time had passed that I could go inside and start cleaning the poison, but I didn't want to give up on Jackson so easily. I was impatient to find out if we would sleep together. "This is it," I told him. "But I forgot—I can't go in."

"Why not?"

"I'm bombing. For fleas."

"Ahhh." He nodded, as if I'd mentioned an old mutual friend. "The herpes of nature."

"I've been drowning them in soap all week."

"Well then," he said, smiling. "What do you want to do?"

I shrugged, hoping he wouldn't offer to drop me off somewhere else.

"Want to come to my place?" he asked.

The offer bloomed before me in a tableau of sweat and naked limbs. "Sure," I said, trying not to sound too excited. "I could do that."

"I live near Vinland. It's about twenty minutes south. That okay?"

"That's fine. I've never heard of it. Sounds like Finland."

"Might as well be." He cranked the radio, and we were off, leaving the tiny holocaust in my apartment behind.

We drove straight back to the country roads we'd just driven, passing fields of scorched grass punctuated by homes with wraparound porches and little man-made ponds that shone like nickels against the sun. Somewhere around the county line, I realized I'd forgotten to take my goldfish, Goldie Prawn, out of the apartment before I bug bombed. Had I been anywhere but in Jackson's truck, I would have cried.

We arrived at his land after a series of turns I couldn't have repeated on my own, yet this disorientation didn't scare me. For some reason, I trusted Jackson.

"This is the Nine," he said, pulling into a gravel drive marked by nothing except an old black mailbox.

"Why the Nine?"

"Ninety acres."

I decided not ask how large or small ninety acres was, settling instead on a notion of a happy medium, a modest fortune of land.

"My dad left it to me when he died," Jackson said. "My brother and I didn't even know he had it. He gave Charlie the house in Lawrence, and I got this. I felt cheated, at first."

"But not anymore?"

"Not a bit."

"Because the house in Lawrence is crappy?"

"No," he said, a hint of defensiveness in his tone. "Because the land is the land, and it's completely mine—was always supposed to be mine. Because if the land were Charlie's he would have ruined it. Would have done something stupid like sell it or develop it or whatever. This place would be a shoe store or a nail salon or something stupid like that."

I curled my fingers into my palms, hiding the French tips I'd just had done.

"And I'm good here. I built myself this little place." He gestured toward what could have easily passed for a garden shed in the city. The structure stood half-hidden by trees, flanked by piles of wood, scrap metal, and cinder blocks. The house itself boasted two little windows. Through the glass I could make out rows of mason jars filled with yellow flowers.

"Like it?" he asked.

I did like it, in the way that people like pictures of places where they would never actually like to live, like tree houses or tents set up on snowy alpine ledges. "It's very rustic," I said. This seemed to satisfy him.

Jackson parked his truck on a little clearing across the way from the house. He looked at me, his eyes bright with something I rarely saw in people anymore. He radiated a naive joy I'd known well during college but that had drained so fast after graduation it now seemed impossible I had ever possessed it. "This here is some of the only wilderness left in Kansas," he said.

"I didn't know Kansas had any wilderness."

"Wilderness is just something nobody's never touched. You don't need mountains or waterfalls to be wild."

"Okay. So. What do you do with a girl out here in the wilderness?" I expected a certain type of answer, the answer all men gave when posed this brand of question. He would offer a wry smile, maybe plop a meaty hand on my thigh and say something like, *We could go inside and I could show you around*, or, *I have a few ideas in mind.*

But Jackson just hopped out and ran a little sprint to the truck bed, from which he extracted two rather large guns. "How about some hunting?" he called.

"Absolutely not," I called back.

"Why not?"

"I don't like to kill things. I'm a vegetarian, remember?"

He snorted. "Hunting don't mean you're gonna kill something. You talk like you'll be good at it."

"It means you're going to try," I said.

"Well then do you want to come with me while I try?"

I did not want to ruin the day. "I guess I could. I like to be out-doors," I lied.

Jackson smiled. "Damn right you do."

We geared up inside his house, where everything was fur and flow-ers. Fauna and flora. Instead of bearskin rugs or cartoonish moose heads he had a pair of stiff, tan leather armchairs and a fleet of potted plants. There were plants by the chairs, by the door, by his bed, which was just a twin mattress on the floor. An elephant's ear kept the little potbellied stove company, its leaves withered and waxy on the hot side. Vines snaked around the posts of lamps and stuck their fingers into his bookshelves, which boasted titles like *The Everything Guide to Tanning and Leatherwork, The Huntsman's Field Guide,* and *Think Like a Turkey.*

He gave me an orange Day-Glo vest and a worn-out baseball cap that read WYOMING GAME AND FISH. "That cap belonged to my father," he said.

I took it, feigning sentimentality, and then smelled it while his back was turned. It stank of old sweat and sunscreen.

Jackson armed himself with one of the guns and then led me away from his house and through a clearing in the trees that I would not have noticed on my own.

"Watch for snakes and don't go wandering," he said. "This place can eat you up."

I doubled my step—he was already several yards in front of me. We pushed deep into the woods until the hum of cicadas overtook the sounds of the little county highway. Minutes later, sunscreen was burning my eyes, and I had approximately one billion mosquito bites. I felt like the dopey younger sister on a Cub Scout trip. My calves ached; the forest had hills you couldn't quite tell were hills until you were climbing them. I wanted water. Jackson was still moving fast, his gaze to the trail. He hadn't looked back since we left his house.

"What are we looking for, anyways?" I asked.

"Anything that moves," he said. "Squirrel, rabbit, deer."

"You kill rabbits? But they're so cute."

"Cute's no reason to live."

"So you eat them? You eat rabbits?"

"In a pinch. They make a decent stew. But what you really want is deer. Enough meat to fill a freezer. Lasts for months. In the winter I sell the jerky at a few gas stations and groceries in the area. But for skins, what you're looking for is bobcat. If it's a holy day you might see a mountain lion."

"There are mountain lions out here?" I quickened my pace.

"You bet. About a week ago, a jogger came close to getting pounced. But he saw the cat coming and played big like they say to do. Cat turned tail."

"I had no idea there were animals that big in Kansas."

"Rumor has it there's a black bear out here. That it came up from Oklahoma, looking for a mate."

"There's bears in Oklahoma?"

"There's all kinds of shit where you wouldn't expect it."

I'd never seen a bear in the wild. Once, right after my parents divorced when I was seven, my dad took me to the Sedgwick County zoo to see a bear. They had a grizzly with some sort of skin disease that made its hair fall out, and people from all over were flocking to see it. My dad told me the bear would be bald, and so I pictured an otherwise normal-looking bear but with a halo of blank skull like my uncle Bill's. When we got there, I was shocked to find that the bear was bald all over. It looked like a monster, with squinty eyes and horrible, pinched cheeks. The skin around its belly hung loose, like an empty trash bag. It was hot outside, and for a moment I genuinely wondered if it was melting. The bear kept trying to hide from the visitors, but it had nowhere to go, and the kids around me kept pelting it with fistfuls of popcorn and sand. I couldn't sleep for a week, and my dad had to remove all of my teddy bears until the terror passed.

"Have you ever seen a hairless bear?" I asked Jackson.

He slowed his gait and turned to look at me. "Actually, yeah. I have. When I was little. It was at the zoo. My dad drove Charlie and me all the way to Wichita."

"We must have seen the same one, then."

"Huh. I haven't thought about that in years. Someone should have put that thing out of its misery."

"I thought it was the scariest thing I'd ever seen. I had nightmares."

"About a bald bear?"

"Sure," I said, nearly catching up to him. "It was spooky."

He laughed, glancing back to shoot me a smile. "That's the funniest thing I've ever heard. Scared of a bald bear. That's like being more afraid of a naked Nazi than a regular Nazi."

Just then, a branch snapped somewhere close. Jackson stopped and then started walking slowly, his movements gaining stealth. I thought of the ex's calico, how she took on a primal fluidity in the presence of mice and laser pointers, slowly bringing herself to the ground where, pupils dilated, she would wait patiently for the moment to attack. Jackson turned to look at me and pressed a finger to his lips. He looked like the type of man you saw in adventure movies, the type of man that women like me—women who got pedicures and appreciated the appeal of small dogs—never had a chance with. It was incredibly attractive, especially coming after the professor, who spent his time writing papers that nobody but his colleagues ever read.

We were at the edge of a clearing, a cluster of pawpaw trees separating us from a half-moon of tall grass. The air was hot and heavy. Jackson leaned close enough that I could smell his deodorant. "Over there," he said. "Two o'clock."

It took me a moment before I saw it—a patch of fur moving through the grass. A deer the color of brown sugar lifted its head. Jackson pulled his gun up to eye level and squinted. "God, she's pretty," he whispered. "Isn't she pretty?"

"What are you doing?" I asked.

He kept squinting, moving the gun as the deer dipped its head into the grass. "Stay quiet."

"You can't," I said.

"What do you mean?"

"I don't want you to. Not while I'm with you."

"Then go somewhere else for a minute."

"Jackson." I felt myself choking up.

He took his gaze from the deer long enough to look at me. "You want me to just let it go? This is hunting, sweetheart. What'd you think we were doing?"

"But, it's just trying to eat." I couldn't help but start crying—he'd called me sweetheart, and not in the good way. But this was how I'd always been with animals. Once, at a house party in college, a friend of mine had a plan to feed a mouse to his pet snake, as a kind of show for the partygoers. The mice were in a little cardboard box, like the ones Happy Meals used to come in, and while nobody was looking I took the box outside and let the mice go. The friend was drunk and annoyed and made me reimburse him for the mice, saying he'd just go buy new ones. But I'd felt victorious, imagining the mice going on to create whole new empires of vermin.

"God, are you crying?" Jackson asked. He put the gun down an inch. "Jesus."

"Jackson," I said. "Please?"

"Oh, hell. Come on." He turned around, brushing past me, and charged back the way we came. I kept after him, nearly running, my heart going nuts. After only a few minutes I realized I needed to pee—bad.

"Jackson, I need to pee."

He slowed down and turned to face me. "Well, go on then. I won't look."

I could tell he was frustrated with me, and for a moment I wished I were a different type of girl, the type of girl who hunted and back-packed and initiated outdoor sex. I walked toward a cluster of thick bushes, just barely out of his line of vision. I squatted down and let go. This was the first time I'd peed outside in years, since my early college days when, as long as you were drunk enough, it was accept-able to go in people's backyards. And then suddenly I saw it—a heap of black fur moving through some reedy trees in the far distance. I stood up as quietly as I could and then squinted to make out what it was, although I already knew.

Just like the deer, the bear raised its head, perhaps sensing that it was being watched. It was not as big as I'd imagined, but still I felt faint. I imagined it noticing me, its eyes taking on an angry recognition. It would charge, leaping through the field separating us until it was on me, all claws and incisors. Jackson would have to carry my body out of the woods.

Holding my breath, I got low, keeping my eyes on the bear. Like this, I crawled back to where Jackson was waiting, a cigarette dangling from his lips.

"Why you crawling like that?" he asked, taking the cigarette from his mouth.

I tried to calm myself, to act natural. "I thought I saw a centipede, but it ran away."

He stubbed the cigarette into the dirt. "You're weird as shit. You know that?"

I smiled up at him, trying to revive whatever connection we'd had before the deer incident. I knew telling him about the bear would make him happy, but I also knew he'd kill it. I was certain. And so I said nothing the rest of the way back to his house, matching his pace and turning back every so often to make sure we weren't being pursued.

"You all right?" Jackson said, once we were back at his house. "You seem frazzled."

I was breathing heavy, my hands on my knees. I looked up at him and nodded, trying to hold my smile. "I'm just out of shape," I said. "Thank you, by the way."

"For what?"

"For not killing that deer."

"I should have," he said, looking back to the woods. "I made a mistake."

"I don't think so. I think what you did was kind."

"Wasn't nothing about kindness. I just don't do so good with people who cry. Makes me feel weird."

"I'm sorry."

"Don't apologize."

I stood up straight and looked at him. He'd put the gun back in his truck, and the way he looked, suddenly defenseless, seemed sweet. Around us, the woods breathed. Despite what had happened, it seemed like a romantic moment. With the ex, our encounters were limited to restaurants and conversations, bedrooms and television shows. The most daring thing we'd ever done was have sex on his kitchen table, an awkward, brief exchange that ended with a constellation of crumbs embedded in my butt cheeks. Never had we stood together in the woods after a hike. Never had we stood amid the threat of a wild animal. Never, come to think of it, had we done anything outdoors together.

Filled with the moment, I made my way to Jackson and kissed him. At first, he grabbed me, holding tight onto my back. But he did not open his mouth, and soon he put a hand on my hip and gently pushed me away. "I'll take you back, now," he said, turning toward the truck.

"What?" I said, my happiness draining.

"Listen, it's been a good day. A fun day, but—"

"You don't want me to stay?"

He looked to his feet. "I'm just feeling out of sorts. With the deer and all." He tried to smile. "I don't know."

My chest tightened. I didn't want to go home. Not to the fleas, to the empty apartment. "I saw a bear out there," I said. "When I was peeing. That's why I was crawling on the ground."

His face went soft. "You what?"

"I saw a bear." I felt everything lighten. I knew that if he found the bear he would kill it. But I was willing to sacrifice it for myself, for my happiness. To stay with Jackson for even a little longer. To delay the drive back to town.

"You sure it was a bear?"

I nodded.

"Why didn't you say something?"

"It happened so fast—I was scared."

He threw a hand in the air and then squeezed his forehead, thinking. Suddenly, he sprang toward the truck and retrieved his gun. Without inviting me along, he took off for the woods. Even if I had wanted to keep up, I knew I wouldn't be able to. He was lean and fast. The woods swallowed him whole in a matter of seconds.

After the shock of his exit wore off, I occupied myself by building miniature huts out of twigs, like I'd done when I was a kid. They didn't stand up for long, but it passed the time. I imagined the creatures that would live in them: ants and spiders and worms. They would throw cocktail parties and raise thousands of children and generally conduct big, important insect lives. When they were old and weary they would put their twig houses up for sale, move to a retirement community made from pinecones. I imagined what Jackson would think. *They already have their own homes*, he would say. *The dirt is their home.* I would protest, explaining that my homes were clearly superior, with windows and doors. Some even had carports.

I was working on a cabana when I heard the shot. A cloud of brown birds exploded from the trees. Then came a moment of total silence, as if every animal in the woods was holding its breath. I thought about running into the woods, trying to find Jackson, but I knew I'd likely get lost, creating even more trouble. And so I waited some more. I waited until the sun oozed behind the trees and the air cooled to the point where I felt chilly for the first time in a long time.

When he came out, he came out empty handed, his eyes red and his skin burned. He was shirtless; the flannel he'd been wearing was balled up under his armpit, visibly covered in blood.

"You killed it," I said.

"Get in the car."

"What happened?"

"Go on, get in." This time his voice was gruff. He threw his gun into the back of the truck. The flannel he tossed onto the ground, not even bothering to look where it landed.

In the car, he turned on a CD, some twangy band I'd never heard of, and tapped the tune on his steering wheel. He was tense. Before he took the exit back to town he looked at me, smiled, and said, "You're sexy as hell, you know that?"

Confused, I gave a weak smile and then turned to watch the fields give way to strip malls and apartment complexes.

At my apartment, he killed the engine and I sat still, waiting for something to happen.

"You okay on the flea front?" he asked.

I nodded.

"You know," he said, "I only kill what I plan to eat. Or use. Just so you know."

"That's nice of you."

"I don't waste anything. Like the Indians."

"They prefer to be called Native Americans, actually."

He smiled and looked down to his pants. "You're too smart for me, honey. I think you're a nice find, though. It would have been nice to be together."

"We are together," I said, growing frustrated. I could feel him getting away. "We're together right now."

This seemed to make him sad. "Why are you trying so hard to force this?" he asked.

"I don't know—maybe because sometimes forcing works? Like, maybe if we just forced it for while, just a few weeks, it would end up clicking?" I could tell I was going to regret everything I'd just told him. I could picture my mother shaking her head.

"Listen, I wish it would work, too, but I know it won't. You know it won't."

"But it could. You don't know. Nobody knows."

"You can't squeeze water from a rock."

"But maybe this isn't a rock. Maybe it's a watermelon. We won't know unless we try."

"Honey, I'm saying I don't much feel like trying."

I did not want to cry, but the tears were there.

He paused, took a deep breath. "You go clean your apartment," he said. "That stuff in those bombs will kill you."

I was about to leave without saying anything, but I felt a sudden wave of anger, of injustice. I'd invested a lot in the day—I'd waited on him in the mind-numbing emptiness of his land. I'd sacrificed the life of a bear for him—for us. Sure, he saved one stupid deer for me, but that wasn't enough. I deserved more. I deserved him. More than anything, I deserved to not go home to an empty apartment filled with poison and memories of a man who did not love me.

"What happened in the woods?" I asked. "Did you kill the bear or not?"

"I didn't kill any stupid bear."

"Sure you did," I said. "Your shirt was covered in blood."

He pursed his lips and let his hands fall into his lap. He wouldn't look at me. "It was a dog," he said. "I thought it was a bear but it was an old Newfoundland I've known for years. Belonged to one of my dad's old buddies who lives up behind the Nine. I knew that dog. His name was Conan. He was a good dog. Smart as hell."

I put a hand on his arm. "Jackson," I said, trying to not let on that I was also feeling relieved, that maybe he did like me, that maybe he was just too upset about the dog to admit it. "Don't beat yourself up," I said. "Doesn't stuff like this happen all the time? With hunting?"

He looked up at me, shrugging my arm off. "No, it doesn't. I had to see my dad's friend cry. You know how embarrassing that is? To see a grown man cry? And then to explain it's because I thought his dog was a *bear*? In Kansas?"

I didn't know what to say. He was looking at me as if I were the one who had gone into the woods and killed that dog. I wondered if he even believed I'd seen a bear. For a moment, I questioned whether I really had, or if it had been Conan all along, and I too had wanted to see a bear, to create a myth out of my small time in the wilderness with Jackson.

"I'm sorry today was so uncomfortable for you," I said, and then I got out. I wanted to slam the door but it was too heavy. Even with all my strength it sort of just creaked shut, and even this didn't do the job—Jackson had to open it from the inside and shut it again himself. By the time I reached my door, I could still feel his truck sitting there. Blowing exhaust.

In my apartment, I wasted no time. I made a beeline to Goldie Prawn's tank and quickly scooped out her body with a Dixie cup. I said a few words as she swirled around the toilet bowl and then told myself to forget about it entirely. It never happened. Next, I took a wet washcloth to everything—the doorknobs, the countertops, the blinds. Whether real or in my head, the poison made me dizzy, and for a while I imagined passing out, how the paramedics would find me days later, brain damaged and foaming at the mouth. "Why was she alone for so long?" they would ask each other, confused as to how a grown woman could die the death of a flea.

While cleaning, I found an old T-shirt the ex used to wear to bed. His initials were written on the tag, as if he'd packed it for summer camp. I remembered something he said to me once, when we first started dating. "I can't tell whether I like you or the *idea* of you," he said. "But then maybe there's no difference."

The sun had barely set when I crawled into bed and found my sheets littered with dead fleas, their tiny corpses like a handful of commas tossed across a blank page.

Not bothering to clean them, I slept until it was Sunday.

In the morning, Maxine wanted to get coffee.

"He's like nobody I've ever met," she said, bringing a latte to her lips. She had a tendency to flutter her eyes when she bragged, and she was doing this now. She and Walt had gone back to her apartment and made love on her sofa. He'd cooked her curry—the best she'd ever had—and then taught her how to say a variety of phrases in Japanese, a novelty he'd picked up while teaching English in Hiroshima. "He can build just about anything," she said. "And he's been *everywhere*. I mean, places I'd never even heard of. Did you know there's a country called Georgia? I didn't believe him. I looked it up as soon as he was gone."

"Sounds like a catch."

"My god, I feel like I've discovered sliced bread or something." She started laughing, a girlish, hysterical laugh that made a few people in the coffee shop turn to look. "I'm sorry," she said, holding a hand over her mouth. "I just keep looking at everyone and thinking: *Did they have sex like this last night?*"

"I'm happy for you," I said, trying very hard not to say something mean.

"What about your guy?" Maxine asked. "Tell me everything."

"He took me home. That's all."

"That's all? He just dropped you off?"

I tried to smile. "We just met them yesterday. What did you expect? A proposal?"

Maxine frowned. "I just hoped you would hit it off like Walt and I did. That maybe we could double-date. I don't know. I'm sorry. I know it's silly—we did just meet them. It's crazy."

"It is. It's very crazy."

"Do you want me to have Walt ask Jackson about you? To have him push things along?"

"God, no. I mean, no. It's okay. Thanks, though. I appreciate it."

"Okay." She looked into her coffee, as if Walt's face were in there. She smiled a dopey smile that made me want to cry. *Why'd yours work and not mine?* I wanted to ask. Instead, I asked, "Have you heard anything about there being bears in Kansas?"

"Like real bears?"

"Yeah. Black bears."

She laughed. "Someone's pulling your leg."

I heard the news on TV about a month later, while waiting for an oil change. I hadn't had a date since Jackson and found myself filling my spare time with unnecessary chores and errands: steam-cleaning my curtains, ironing clothes that didn't fit me anymore. One day I drove all the way to a hardware store in Topeka just to buy a new shower-head—I'd gotten it into my mind that the old one was contaminated with poison. When there was nothing left to do, I vacuumed my carpet, imaging whole cities of fleas spiraling up into the tube.

It was the six o'clock news and the anchors donned droopy-eyed expressions to prove their sadness. An eleven-year-old girl had been mauled in her grandmother's backyard, just a few miles outside of Vinland. The little girl, who had lost a leg and an eye, had been out feeding her grandmother's mastiffs. Upon finding the bear, and her mangled granddaughter, the grandmother grabbed a rifle and fired seven bullets. Two of them entered the black bear's brain.

The grandmother was now on the news, discussing the incident with a pretty, wide-eyed news anchor. The grandmother had a mane of white hair and a small, puckered mouth. "Terrible monsters, bears," she said, scowling into the anchor's microphone. "What they did to my poor baby. They should be ashamed of themselves. The whole species. Wish there were more of them out here. I'd shoot a whole family of 'em if I could. Have myself a good ole Berenstain Bear massacre. Hang their big fat heads in a row above my oven." She pursed her lips into a tight smile, savoring the thought of it.

The mechanic at the register laughed. "God, what a nut, huh?"

I ignored him and kept watching, trying not to think about Jackson—where he was, what he might be doing. Maxine was having a birthday party the next weekend, and she'd invited him along as company for Walt. I didn't like to think about how many times I'd tried on the dress I planned to wear to the party, or the three miles I'd started to run every evening, through the bug-infested woods near the levy.

The news anchor was talking now, listing off facts about the accident, perhaps to deflect from the grandmother's monologue. But the camera stayed on the grandmother, who kept smiling and twitching her little pink mouth excitedly, as if she was there to receive an award.

Acknowledgments

To my friends and Avalonians, thank you for your continual love and support and for all the days of playing make-believe. To my Kansas teachers: Monica Patino, John Steere, Debra Cole, Judy Goodpasture, Gregg Schwendner, Adam Desnoyers, Laura Moriarty, Megan Kaminski, and Mary Klayder, thank you for believing in me and encouraging my writing when I was just a pipsqueak.

Thank you to Yiyun Li, Annie Liontas, and Lynn Freed for your invaluable guidance, wisdom, and perhaps most importantly, your sense of humor. How lucky am I to have found such a powerhouse team of women? Thanks also to Jacob Garber, Emma Boyce, Christina Turner, and my cohort at UC Davis for helping to inspire and shape these stories. The alternate title will always be *The Jacob Stories*.

Thank you to Lee K. Abbott and Courtney Denney for your close eye and generous attention, and to the lovely people at the University of Georgia Press, especially Beth Snead and Jon Davies, for working with me despite mountain-related technical difficulties.

To Pam Houston: thank you, for everything. But especially the hikes.

Finally, thank you to my mother, Susan, who would give me the moon if she could, only so I could give it back. This book is for you. Every word is always for you.

THE FLANNERY O'CONNOR AWARD FOR SHORT FICTION

David Walton, *Evening Out*
Leigh Allison Wilson, *From the Bottom Up*
Sandra Thompson, *Close-Ups*
Susan Neville, *The Invention of Flight*
Mary Hood, *How Far She Went*
François Camoin, *Why Men Are Afraid of Women*
Molly Giles, *Rough Translations*
Daniel Curley, *Living with Snakes*
Peter Meinke, *The Piano Tuner*
Tony Ardizzone, *The Evening News*
Salvatore La Puma, *The Boys of Bensonhurst*
Melissa Pritchard, *Spirit Seizures*
Philip F. Deaver, *Silent Retreats*
Gail Galloway Adams, *The Purchase of Order*
Carole L. Glickfeld, *Useful Gifts*
Antonya Nelson, *The Expendables*
Nancy Zafris, *The People I Know*
Debra Monroe, *The Source of Trouble*
Robert H. Abel, *Ghost Traps*
T. M. McNally, *Low Flying Aircraft*
Alfred DePew, *The Melancholy of Departure*
Dennis Hathaway, *The Consequences of Desire*
Rita Ciresi, *Mother Rocket*
Dianne Nelson, *A Brief History of Male Nudes in America*
Christopher McIlroy, *All My Relations*
Alyce Miller, *The Nature of Longing*
Carol Lee Lorenzo, *Nervous Dancer*
C. M. Mayo, *Sky over El Nido*
Wendy Brenner, *Large Animals in Everyday Life*
Paul Rawlins, *No Lie Like Love*
Harvey Grossinger, *The Quarry*
Ha Jin, *Under the Red Flag*
Andy Plattner, *Winter Money*
Frank Soos, *Unified Field Theory*
Mary Clyde, *Survival Rates*
Hester Kaplan, *The Edge of Marriage*

CPSIA information can be obtained
at www.ICGtesting.com
Printed in the USA
LVHW041920260220
648294LV00004B/491